D0940520

THE RAT

a novel by

Merrill Wautlet

L.A.B., Shreveport, Louisiana

Copyright © 2019 by Merrill Wautlet
Edited by Andrew Mercer and Gary Prechter

All rights reserved. This book, or parts thereof, may not be reproduced without permission from the copyright holder.

Published in the United States of America by
L.A.B. Printing and Office Supply

First edition: September, 2019

10 9 8 7 6 5 4 3 2 1

ISBN: 978-0-578-61545-5

DEDICATIONS

To the boards, management teams, and staffs at St. Mary's Residential Training School and Holy Angels Residential Facility, two remarkable institutions who perform miracles every day.

To M.C. and Andrew, who inspire me with their unconditional love, their approach to life, and the way they treat all the people they meet. They are my role models.

"Man plans. God laughs."

"Why fit in when you were born to stand out?"
Dr. Seuss

CONTENTS

PROLOGUE

Mike Waters sat in shock as the pediatric psychiatrist droned on with his diagnosis. As the color drained from Mike's face, he kept repeating a single word over and over again in his head. Autism.

"Look at him." The doctor continued to point out all of Mike's son's flaws with steely precision. "He doesn't make eye contact. He isn't talking yet and he has poor receptive language skills. He is totally oblivious to what is going on in here right now. Look how he is wandering around the room."

The cold delivery pissed off Mike. He could appreciate physicians being detached to avoid their own emotional heartache, but this guy was being an asshole. It was almost as if he felt compelled to ram home all the deficiencies Mike's son had in such a way to not only inform, but also take away hope.

Mike tried to gather himself. His wife, Jenny, could not make the appointment so he had to deal with this doctor without her calming influence. Mike suspected that Jenny had already reached this conclusion, and that may have been why he was now here alone. He looked at the doctor and spoke. "What are our options?"

"He has behavior issues," the doctor replied. "We will have to try different drug combinations to alleviate his aggressive tendencies." The doctor didn't even bother to look at Mike. He just stared at his note pad as he scribbled his observations. The office decor was in contrast to the physician's demeanor. It was fashioned in the style of a study you would find in a fine home. A beautiful desk, built-in bookshelves, and an oriental rug adorned the wood floors beneath it. It was warm and inviting, but the doctor was not.

"Drugs!" Mike exclaimed. "Are there no other avenues we can pursue?" At that point the doctor looked at Mike and stared intently at him. It was only for a moment but it seemed much longer before the doctor continued. "This boy is going to require significant early intervention and a drug protocol will have to be a part of that. You have to understand I'm fairly certain he is intellectually disabled, too. He is probably never going to speak. He may even have to be institutionalized." Upon finishing his sentence, he rose from his chair, walked to his bookcase and retrieved a hefty tome. Turning to Mike, the doctor thrust the book at him. On the cover Mike saw the words "Autism and Spectrum Disorder." The doctor then barked a command, "Read this. Some of it may be over your head but it will reaffirm what we talked about today. This is just a loan. I want it back when you are done."

Mike rose from his chair. He went over and gently took his two-and-a-half-year-old son by the hand. As he left the office, Mike slammed the door behind him.

CHAPTER ONE
The Mission

The black Ford Explorer cruised slowly. This was the vehicle of choice for the agency because of their roominess, ample storage, and powerful engine. They were also still closely associated with law enforcement, which kept people at bay, especially at night. The lightly tinted windows added an aura of authority to the vehicle. Poor illumination was offered by the lights on the street, which were lifeless save for a pack of dogs sniffing through garbage that had spilled from a container. This part of the Chicagoland metro area was residential and at this hour, its inhabitants were by and large asleep.

Edward Brooks steered the vehicle with his left hand, his right hand grasping a small foam cup of coffee. A large man, Brooks' hand practically enveloped the small receptacle. He took slow sips as he continued to drive. Dr. Joseph Myers sat beside him, gazing at an illuminated iPad on his lap, struggling to absorb the data contained on its screen. A man of slight build, Myers was a contrast to the hulking Brooks. Both men were in their early fifties. Brooks' physique was still firm but the closely cropped beard that covered his large jaw was speckled with white and gray. Myers was squinting behind his glasses, occasionally running a hand through his receding hairline.

In the back seat sat a solitary figure. His blond hair seemed to shimmer as the glow from the street lights struck it through the darkened glass.

His body was rigid and erect, hands at his sides resting on the seat. He was fastened securely with a seat belt. His blue eyes were focused straight ahead and his face was devoid of any expression. He had been that way since the three of them had left the field office located on the outskirts of the city limits of Chicago an hour earlier. Brooks had been on numerous assignments with his backseat passenger over the past two years. He was accustomed to his stoic behavior. Myers was accompanying the pair for the first time.

"Is he always like this?" Myers asked.

"Always," Brooks replied, without offering any additional explanation.

Myers then picked up some notes he had jotted down on a paper tablet. He was still old school in some ways, and the familiar feel of pressing a pen to paper was a hard habit to break. The notes consisted of the basic components of the assignment along with contingencies for anything they might encounter that would cause a deviation from the plan. Myers looked back up at Brooks. "We just drop him off, drive to our designated waiting area, and then hope he comes back?"

"That is correct," Brooks replied with a steady voice.

Myers persisted, his voice rising. "The boy has never been here before! How will he find his way?"

Brooks' face frowned slightly. He preferred working alone and Myers' probing questions were starting to annoy him. He decided to deal with the good doctor in a decisive manner.

Brooks pulled the car to the curb. As the engine idled Brooks stared at Myers. "Andre has been through a myriad of simulations relating to this particular assignment. He knows how to get into the building and he knows how to get out. Once he exits he will follow the path that has been ingrained in him through the repetitive nature of his training. He doesn't have to know where he is to find us. He only needs to know how many steps between left turns and right turns and he knows the car."

Myers shook his head in disbelief. "How does he react to unexpected occurrences?"

Brooks glared at Myers. "Did you read the file on Andre?"

Myers recoiled slightly. He was not a field agent. He was an academic and a physician with a background in both psychology and psychiatry. His path to the agency was a trail that had begun with his own substance abuse. His private practice gone, the opportunity to work with a covert government agency was intriguing. Tonight, however, was something from a science fiction novel.

He had indeed read the file on Andre Waters, but was skeptical of its contents. His purpose here was to evaluate Andre after he had finished his assignment. On previous missions formal evaluations had been conducted on Andre upon his return to headquarters, but there had never been an examination by a physician immediately after the completion of an assignment. "I read it, Brooks, but it just seemed so far-fetched. I mean, how old is this kid? Nine? Ten?"

A slight smile pierced Brooks' lips. He, too, had once questioned how effective a child could be in their line of work. Their first assignment together changed all of that. "I first met Andre over two years ago. We were in D.C. This agency was in a period of transition. Homeland Security may be the official anti-terrorism arm, but many of the real accomplishments have been achieved by the work this department does. I was briefed on Andre before I met him. They brought him into the warehouse that we had rented as our base. He just walked to the car and got in. I said 'hello' and it was as though I was not even there. He was so young it shocked me. He could not have weighed more than fifty pounds. My instructions were to go to a location in the city that we believed a terrorist cell was operating from. My only orders were to drop off Andre and then wait."

Brooks pulled slowly from the curb. He came to an intersection. The light was red. He ran it. At three o'clock in the morning, there were no police or cars to be concerned with. He began to speak again. "I sat at my assigned location for an hour. I was not sure how long it was going to take him to complete his mission so I used my iPad to send an encrypted message asking when the kid should be finishing up. The response I got was that if Andre has noticed any activity inside the house that was not consistent with his training he would hold his position. I was to wait until he returned." Brooks took a deep breath. It was as if he was reliving the experience all over again. "When Andre left the car he had inserted himself into a crevice of the house partially concealed by debris. He had to crouch into a ball, press against the wall, and stay there until he saw it was clear or was given a command to move. If needed, a signal would be transmitted through a band on his wrist. It vibrates when turned on and measures his vital signs."

Myers listened intently, mesmerized by Brooks' monologue. Brooks continued. "I learned that this whole mission was supposed to take less than thirty minutes. It had now been an hour and that kid had not moved. He stayed in that spot, crouched up in a ball, for almost six hours. His pulse and rate of breathing were so calm I thought he had fallen asleep. Finally I was ordered to give the go ahead. He infiltrated the house, obtained the information he was assigned to get on a flash drive, and he returned to the car."

Myers jaw went slack. "What was his condition? Was he rattled at all?"

"The kid was fine. He seemed to appear out of nowhere. He came to the car and got in, handed me the flash drive and curled up on the back seat and went to sleep. We had gotten there at approximately eleven o'clock in the evening. By the time he returned it was a little after five in the morning. It was damn cold out there but he looked fine."

Brooks' eyebrows arched. "We later learned that he met with resistance inside the house, which apparently he must have suspected would happen and was the reason he waited."

Myers was dumbfounded. "What did he do? What happened to the people he encountered?"

"Given the confidential nature of his very existence, all information on Andre's activities are given on a need-to-know basis. I do know that a guy was hauled out of that house and taken to the hospital. Their computers are not networked so hacking is a challenge. Andre defeats that by getting data right off their hard drives. That flash drive he obtained allowed us to arrest thirty extremists and stop five planned attacks on soft targets here in the U.S. We soon realized that we could use this application on not only terrorists but also drug cartels, organized crime, even white-collar cases. If something needs to be obtained, we had the ability now to go and get it. However, our main focus is still to seek and find sleeper terrorist cells, wherever they exist."

Myers looked up at Brooks. "In those situations, without a warrant, none of that evidence is admissible in court. What good is it to you?"

Brooks rolled his eyes. "We have ways around that."

Myers turned around and looked at Andre. "So this kid has an autistic diagnosis and is scooped up out of nowhere and turned into some sort of master thief. How does that happen? What about his parents?"

Brooks was curt. "That is classified and I would suggest strongly that you leave it at that."

The car pulled to a stop in front of a closed gas station. It was unseasonably warm for upstate Illinois in April and there was a gentle breeze blowing. Brooks lowered the car windows. Myers again looked at Andre. "Does he know we are talking about him?"

"Who knows?" Brooks said with a shrug. "If you ask me I think he knows exactly what is happening but he sure as hell never lets on."

They were ahead of schedule. Brooks reached into his center console and pulled out a cellophane bag. Its contents contained an apple, two pretzel rods, and a small six-ounce can of caffeine-free Coke.

"Here you go, Blondie." Brooks handed the contents to Andre. He began to eat and drink carefully, taking slow deliberate bites and sips.

"He's a healthy eater," Myers remarked.

"He loves that stuff. I tried to give him some candy once and he pushed it back at me. The guys at HQ said he came in like that. He just always seemed to prefer healthy foods, especially fruit. The only deviation is the Coke. Other than that, it's mainly fruit and lean meat. He loves mayonnaise. That kid will eat pizza with mayo on it. Once he figured out where the kitchen was he would sneak in and take food back to his room. He had a stash set up under his bed. One of the operatives called him a little rat and it stuck and became his code name."

Suddenly an empty Coke can was thrust in Brooks' face followed by an apple core and an empty cellophane bag. "Feel better dude?" Brooks asked, not expecting an answer.

Brooks checked his watch. It was now three-thirty. The target was in sight—a brownstone. No lights were on. Parked cars lined both sides of the street. Brooks leaned over the back seat. "Okay man, let's check you out." Brooks was ensuring that Andre's suit was fitted properly.

"Put your mask on."

Andre then reached on the seat and grabbed his mask, pulling it over his head. The mask covered his entire face. The eye openings were covered with plastic lenses. He then put his gloves on. With no prompting, Andre reached behind his head and pulled an attached hood over it.

Brooks began to speak. "The hood has no practical purpose. It just calms him. When we first tried to fit him for the suit, it really caused a lot of behaviors. Then one of the guys that worked with him recalled that Andre always pulled his hood on when he wore a hoodie sweatshirt or jacket. So we added a hood and we had no more problems."

The whole suit was black and lightweight. Warm in the winter and cool in the summer. The feet and gloves were fitted with material that could grip almost any surface, and the fabric was tear resistant and water proof. The lenses were infrared but would adjust to any light to allow clear vision. The glove that covered Andre's left hand and wrist contained the monitoring device that could give him his signal as well as monitor his heart rate. On the suit was a flap that sealed with adhesive strips. It was situated on Andre's stomach and it served as a pouch to place whatever he might retrieve, thus leaving his hands free. Inside the pouch was a flash drive secured by a small piece of Velcro.

"What was he like when he was first brought in?" Myers asked.

"He was very difficult," Brooks answered. "He would throw tantrums, hit himself about his head with his fists, and bang his head on the wall. The worst was the excrement. He would have bowel movements and smear crap everywhere. After a while, they were able to get him settled. His room has no pictures and they soundproofed and padded the walls. Apparently, he was sensitive to noise and other types of stimulation.

"He has a TV with a DVD player and an internet connection. He watches DVDs and digital videos, mainly those kid musicals. He also has some rubber balls and UNO cards. They have to be Sesame Street UNO cards or he won't have anything to do with them. You wouldn't believe how many guys from the office buy those damn things when they see them."

Brooks paused for a moment, then continued. "The kid was placed on a strict routine that helped ease his transition. He ate, slept, and woke up at the same time every day, seven days a week. He went through some serious training. Twelve hours a day was the norm and he got the full load, gymnastics, martial arts, and swimming. Essentially Andre has been trained to react to any events that could occur during an assignment."

Suddenly Brooks straightened forward. An encrypted message came over the iPad situated on the console between himself and Myers.

"It's time." Brooks turned and looked at Andre. "Go," he said in a controlled voice. Andre unbuckled his seat belt, opened the car door, and ventured into the night air.

The Rat

CHAPTER TWO
Reflection

David Wilson paced the floor of his office. He often wondered what the view would be if he had an office in a high-rise building. His D.C. digs were well appointed but the code restrictions on building height in the nation's capital meant that his view was less than spectacular. His office looked more like a den than a work place. It had a Persian rug along with a plush sofa, accompanied by two oversized stuffed chairs. A fireplace was situated inside the northern wall, although on this warm night it was not in use. The office was surrounded by an ornate series of shelves fully stocked with volumes of classic literature. A full bar sat against another wall and a flat screen television was mounted up high near a corner of the room.

He had a large desk with a side table that had two large computer monitors perched atop it. One monitor had a map with a small image moving on it. It was the Ford Explorer, which was being tracked using a global positioning system that was installed on it. The other was full of unopened e-mails. On the television was The Weather Channel.

Upon accepting the assignment, Wilson demanded that he have an office in the city with no military ties to it. A sign on the front door read "Terrebonne Consulting," an homage to the parish of his birth. It maintained consistency with the story he gave others when asked about his occupation. Beneath that title were the admonishments "By Appointment Only" and "No Soliciting."

Wilson never could sleep on a night when Andre was on assignment. Even though he had confidence in Andre's training and abilities, he was still unable to rest. The thought that Andre was only a ten-year-old would creep in his head and fester like a wound. Wilson despised feeling guilty. Abducting Andre and converting him into a thief and spy had proven to be a brilliant move. Wilson's agency had excelled in its early years to infiltrate and disrupt the activities of various terrorist cells located around the country. Despite that success, he had come under criticism for the use of excessive force by his recruits. Once he began using the Rat, he had obtained more information and made more arrests in the past two years than he had in the previous five. Most important was that Andre's thefts were undetectable, and as such created confusion among the targets as they wondered how files and stored computer data had disappeared without a trace.

Wilson moved his lanky six-foot-five frame towards his desk. He removed his glasses and wiped the lenses in a rhythm born of habit. His brown hair was tussled and unkempt. Like a waking dream, it happened again. David's thoughts began to center on his cousin Jenny.

Wilson had left his home years ago. Houma, Louisiana, was a town that had a vibrant bounce that reflected its Cajun heritage. Surrounded by bayous and near the Gulf of Mexico, the town revolved around oil and routinely boomed and busted in concert with the cyclical nature of the business. For David it was a distant place, far removed from the circumstance of his current life.

Wilson had grown weary of hearing how he was not reaching his potential. School had been boring, Houma was boring, so he left. He joined the Navy. It was there that his intellect unleashed itself. After a series of evaluations and tests, he soon found himself working in intelligence. As the years passed, he rose in rank and eventually worked with both the FBI and CIA. When approached about forming a maverick agency to secretly combat terrorism on U.S. soil, Wilson leapt at the opportunity. He was now his own boss. Toiling in secrecy was not a concern, as he did not wish for celebrity. His aphrodisiacs were control and power.

It was not an easy assignment. To covertly recruit personnel, develop an infrastructure, and combat terrorist activity was daunting. The veil of secrecy was essential because Homeland Security wanted results but felt constrained by the laws of the land. The very laws that protected people's freedoms also provided shelter for terrorists and criminals. Even the Patriot Act was not enough. Wilson's job was to use data provided by Homeland Security, the FBI, and the CIA, and stop or eliminate terrorists by whatever means necessary.

At first, it seemed simple enough. Wilson scoured personnel files searching for men who were patriots but had been run out of their particular branch of the service. Their offenses ranged from insubordination to wrongful use of deadly force. Wilson needed men who had no remorse and who would be eager to get back into action. He also needed people who could manage the technology needed to run an operation the size and scope of this, as their activities would be exclusively mobile. To be housed in any one place for any length of time risked discovery.

The installation of the framework of the agency took almost two years. Recruiting the needed personnel took longer than anticipated. Setting up shell corporations to lease property and buy equipment also took time. Finally, they were ready to act and the results were spectacular. Wilson's field agents were highly skilled in the art of combat and they carried out their assignments with gruesome efficiency. The body count was managed with leaks to the press and law enforcement that created plausible causes that averted suspicion from any government agency. Two years later a new

President was elected and his desires were clear. Not knowing of the effectiveness of the agency, or even its existence, he demanded accountability. Europe was still awash in bombings and death and the new commander-in-chief wanted to prove to Americans that they were safe. The new head of Homeland Security now had to make a splash publicly. While Wilson's job ultimately remained secure, and his identity still concealed, it all came with a price. His agency now had to execute raids that resulted in arrests and capture of terrorists, not body bags disposed of discreetly or via false information to the police. They had to secure data, not kill the enemy, and then filter it discreetly to those agencies that operated in the sunshine. The government had to be seen as being effective and humane for the people of the nation. Wilson's men were now obsolete as their forté was combat, not theft. He knew that he would have to adapt his agency's style, and possibly its personnel, if he was going to keep his current position in this new administration. He also found himself with a budget for the first time. Like any CEO, he had to keep costs down.

When Wilson returned to Houma five years ago for his sister's wedding, he had been away for almost two decades. He dodged questions about his occupation, merely responding that he was a consultant. His family and friends in Houma, just happy to see him, never persisted further regarding the details of his personal and professional lives. Wilson had not kept up with family events. There were the occasional phone calls home, but for the most part, he had been staying in contact as a service to his mother. He called more often after his father died, but his efforts at staying connected were haphazard at best. He had not even attended his father's funeral. As such, this visit home was like a surreal experience—familiar faces and places out of context with no real meaning to him. It did not matter who his sister was marrying, or that she was getting married at all. Wilson was going to be there because his mother had pleaded so passionately that he be in attendance. She had spoken at length that it would mean so much to his sister and her. The worst part for him was that he would have to stand in for his father and give his sister away.

The church was filled to capacity. Wilson's maternal grandfather had been a person of great importance in the community and his father had prospered in part because of that. His sister had made her debut and served as queen of the local Mardi Gras carnival organization. While the club was not as prestigious as the old-line carnival krewes in New Orleans, to the good people of Houma the designations were no less significant.

Wilson had purposely come into town at the latest possible date to avoid all the various parties, teas, and showers that were a part of a wedding in southern Louisiana. He had entered the church and stood by his mother, taking cues from her as people filed in, faces he no longer recognized and names he no longer remembered.

Jenny and Mike Waters had arrived at the church with Mike holding Andre by the hand. Jenny's father was David's uncle and his mother quickly identified the couple for him. She told him how Jenny was a special education teacher and that Mike, a banker, was from New Orleans. She then focused on Andre. The small wiry boy was five years old and autistic. She spoke of how difficult it had been for Jenny and Mike, coming to terms with Andre's diagnosis and wading through the vast array of therapies that were being tried to treat his condition.

At that moment, with no warning, Andre bolted from his father. He moved swiftly yet deliberately down the aisle and then moved through a pew, deftly stepping on or around the kneelers, as he headed towards the wall of the church.

The Cathedral of St. Francis De Sales was an old gothic revival style church. The Catholic Parish had been in existence since 1847 and the first church was built in 1848. The structure was rebuilt in 1938 because of hurricane damage sustained years earlier. It had columns, statues, and ornate stained glass windows. Andre immediately affixed himself to one of the columns and began to climb. The wedding guests became hushed as all eyes fixed on the child. Gasps and cries erupted as he moved effortlessly up the smooth surface, clinging to it magically as it arched up towards the high ceiling.

David too was transfixed, but not by Andre. He was astonished as Jenny and Mike calmly moved towards the column. They seemed neither worried nor afraid as their child climbed further. Andre reached a stone edifice adorned with the body of an arch-angel, standing guard with its sword in the air. Andre approached the angel and, while leaning perilously back, grasped its face in his hands, staring at it. He then leaned forward and began smelling its stone visage.

Some forty feet below Mike and Jenny stood at the base of the pillar. Jenny looked at Mike. "I thought you had him?"

Mike, still staring up at Andre replied, "Me too. Hey Buddy, you have had your fun. Come down now."

Andre looked down at his father. He then placed first one hand and then the other on the angel's outstretched arm. He began to swing casually and then he let go of the statue's arm with one hand, dangling above the hushed throng below. He was grinning as he began alternating hands, each movement causing cries of fear to emerge from the wedding guests.

"I think he just likes to torment me," Mike said as a slight frown crossed his face.

Jenny's face, now stern, was awash not with fear, but rather with embarrassment. She affixed a steely glare on Andre. "You get down here right now!" Her voice echoed throughout the cavernous church.

At the sound of his mother's voice Andre stopped dangling. He placed his feet at the base of the angel and began to descend the pillar. As quickly as he had gone up he was now back on the ground. He turned around to face his parents. Jenny offered her hand and they walked calmly towards an empty pew, as if nothing had happened at all.

The people inside the church who had just witnessed the spectacle were still overcome with shock, but all managed to conceal their concerns and fear. David Wilson was in awe. He had never seen anything like that in his life!

Wilson paused as if to catch his breath from the memory of the first time he came across Andre. He walked to a window and stared down at the traffic below, watching cars maneuver through the busy streets of Washington. His mind drifted again.

His sister's wedding reception was an outdoor affair held at the plantation home of a family friend. A three-piece Cajun band played as guests filed through the buffet line. The catered cuisine was indigenous to the area. Jambalaya, gumbo, along with traditional foods such as carved roast beef and ham. Liquor, wine, and beer flowed abundantly as people danced and conversed.

David recalled strolling casually towards Jenny and Mike. They had positioned themselves away from the crowd, which allowed Andre to casually inspect the various flowers and plants that adorned the property. He remembered embracing Jenny and beginning the ritual of small talk. It had occurred to him earlier that his cousin had been an accomplished gymnast in her youth. She had garnered many awards before leaving the sport in her early teens. In speaking with Jenny, he learned that the boy's father had played on a state championship basketball team in high school. Andre's special talent appeared to be a directly associated with his gene pool.

Wilson had coerced information from Jenny about Andre. She related that because she taught special education, she had noticed Andre's autistic tendencies well before his second birthday. She spoke of the absence of language, how he had never showed fear, and needed a strict routine to function. Wilson also learned that the child had demonstrated unbelievable coordination and reflexes at an early age. He had begun walking around fifteen months and was swimming by age three. She recounted the anxiety of watching him scale trees and houses and then the relief as he came down unhurt.

"We know what Andre is capable of," Jenny had said. "I know that the church incident was scary to most of the people in there but Mike and I knew he was in control and would be fine. If there hadn't been so many people inside, we probably would have let him play a while longer," Jenny said with a chuckle. "Frankly, that was something we had never seen him do before, but he has never attempted a physical stunt without succeeding. One time at home, he stood on the railing at the top of the stairs with his back to the open stairwell. He was on his toes touching the ceiling fan. The blade popped his fingers and he pulled back and lost his balance. As he fell, he contorted in the air, landed on his feet and hands on the stairs. It all happened so fast I didn't have time to be scared. He just instinctively seems to know what to do."

Jenny went on about Andre's lack of fear. How he enjoyed roller coasters and other thrill rides. She spoke of his love of long car trips and how he would sit and stare out of the window for hours just soaking in the scenery. She also revealed that Andre had a high tolerance for pain. He seldom ever cried, even when he was in apparent discomfort.

Wilson's mind returned to the present, his guilt replaced by a sense of accomplishment. He had taken a disabled child and through hours of training, had molded him into a patriot. A boy who was destined to be a burden to society had been converted into a valuable asset. Wilson felt smug as he settled into his plush office chair.

CHAPTER THREE
Jenny

Jenny Waters placed her key in the front door dead bolt and unlocked it to retrieve the morning paper resting on her front porch. There was something comforting to her about holding an actual newspaper instead of reading it online. Always an early riser, she found herself sleeping less and less.

The Acadian style home she and Mike owned was tranquilly set amidst scores of pine trees. The Waters had bought the house after Andre had been diagnosed with autism. The move to St. Tammany Parish was tied to Andre's condition. He would need good public schools and the St. Tammany Parish school district was considered the best in Louisiana. Jenny easily found work, as special education teachers were in high demand. Mike also procured employment at a local bank. They had made all the right moves and were on course to build a new life twenty-four miles from New Orleans on the north shore of Lake Pontchartrain.

Andre had been placed in a preschool class for children with special needs. Even after two years of intense early intervention, at age four he was still not completely toilet trained and was making no progress in his language development.

Andre's teachers and therapists had all said the same thing. They believed Andre could learn to use language to some degree as well as learn to use the toilet. Their assessment was that he just wasn't ready, and only until he wanted to achieve those goals would any progress be made. The teachers and therapists all spoke of his strong will and how he seemed to be challenging them.

With her paper in hand she closed the door and moved towards the kitchen, the pine floors creaking as she walked. She grabbed the television remote and began making coffee. A cable news channel appeared on the television screen. The TV was on not for entertainment but for noise. Even with Mike due to wake up in a couple of hours, she knew conversation would not be forthcoming. Neither had much to say to the other since Andre's abduction. They were equally devastated but grieved differently. Each imagined versions of the potential horrors that may have befallen Andre. Was he dead or alive?

It had been five years since he was taken. The abduction had made national news. The school bus Andre was on had been intercepted. As it traveled a quiet road, two black sedans blockaded it, one from the front with the other coming from behind. Two men armed with handguns had entered the bus. They were dressed all in black and they wore hoods to conceal their faces. Once inside they went directly to Andre, grasped his hand and left. They blew out a tire on the bus and disappeared. The event was so well coordinated that it was estimated it took less than three minutes from start to finish. The Waters were not rich so ransom was ruled out. They also were never contacted by anyone. Their child was taken for no apparent reason.

Due to the nature of the kidnapping, the Waters were investigated thoroughly by various arms of law enforcement. It was unbearable. First, their child was taken. Then they were treated as suspects. After months of questions and scrutiny, the Waters were absolved, but the total trauma had taken its toll. Jenny had been stoic during the endless questions and probes. She seemed to withdraw to a private place within herself, enduring the process with as much dignity as she could muster. Her husband was another matter. Mike Waters, a large man standing six foot two and weighing well over two hundred pounds, had never been comfortable with the efforts of law enforcement to find his son and took great umbrage at being a suspect. Several times during routine questioning his emotions got the best of him. At one point during a session with two FBI agents, he became enraged and launched himself over a table at them. The encounter left him with a broken arm but in a strange way, it helped convince the authorities that the parents indeed had nothing to do with the disappearance of their only son. Their grief was too profound. That, combined with the absence of incrimination through cell phone records, e-mails, or cash transactions of meaningful significance, ultimately caused them not to be charged. The next assumption was an illegal adoption ring kidnapping, and while the case remained open, it was soon relegated to a subordinated status as other priorities emerged.

After two years, Mike wanted to move back to New Orleans. He felt like their present home and community carried too many memories. However, Jenny wanted to stay. Her reason was Andre. She harbored a hope that he might one day return. While Mike had visions of his son being raped, tortured, or killed, Jenny felt that he was being cared for, that someone or something had her son for a reason, and that ultimately he might yet come home. She rationalized that this was the only home her son would know and that they had to stay, forever if necessary.

She remembered taking Andre to her classroom. She had let him explore the room and line up objects in the intricate patterns he did with his toys at home. This wasn't creative play but rather a type of obsessive-compulsive disorder that drove him to create those patterns. To redirect Andre she had produced a map of the United States. She had taken Andre's hand and would place his finger in the state of Louisiana just above the massive lake that separated New Orleans from St. Tammany. "Home," she used to say. "This is where we live." Jenny recalled how Andre had a keen sense of direction. He knew the way to the store, the bank, even his grandparents' house. Jenny knew this because to deviate from the routine of these trips in any way would cause Andre to become enraged and begin to beat himself about his head and face as he screamed relentlessly. As such, they had to stay put. If Andre could get home, this was the place he would come to.

Jenny diligently tried to solve problems associated with Andre's limitations. In the beginning, dealing with Andre's disability was difficult, and at times almost impossible.

Andre's initial diagnosis was autism and intellectual disability. He was also classified as having insomnia and self-abusive behavior. He was non-verbal and resisted all efforts to learn sign language. He chose not to initiate interaction with his peers or his parents. He preferred to be alone, usually stacking objects or laying them out in carefully spaced intricate patterns. To force therapies on him only made him irritated, with episodes of tantrums and self-abuse ensuing. When that happened, only long car rides could calm him or help him fall asleep. His upper and lower extremity strengths were normal, as were his hearing and eyesight. He could use both hands cooperatively in bilateral activities and he possessed a keen sense of smell. He used a mature grasp to manipulate items and his equilibrium was extraordinary. He never seemed to lose his balance or fall, no matter what the exercise. He could also swim like a fish.

Jenny had trouble accepting the intellectual disability label. Andre could identify objects from pictures and he seemed to have a comprehensive receptive vocabulary, as he would adhere to instructions and commands. The whole magnitude of his condition was staggering. Over one-and-a-half million people were reportedly diagnosed with some form of autism spectrum disorder, with fifty children a day being identified. Jenny had gone her whole life not knowing a single person with the condition and now it seemed like she was being bombarded with information and predictions of what her life would be like with her son.

Andre was stubborn and had a will of iron. If he was not inclined to do a task, no amount of prompting would make him comply. He scored poorly on the Slosson intelligence test, obtaining a mental age of one year ten months at age four. The Stanford-Binet test offered similar results.

Jenny eventually decided that categorizing Andre based on scientific labels was not going to help her or her son. She decided to accept him as his own person, and committed herself to helping him reach his potential, whatever that was.

Mike chose to insulate himself from the barrage of doctor's visits and tests. He was loving and attentive to Andre, but did nothing to educate himself on his son's condition. He placed himself in a state of denial, hoping that someday Andre would simply emerge from his shell.

This caused stress for Jenny. She felt it was unfair that Mike would choose to stay in his dream world while she was left to make all the difficult decisions on Andre's care. She attended all the Individual Evaluation Plan meetings and all the parent-teacher conferences. She had to deal with all the doctor visits and therapy sessions.

She tried to tell Mike how she felt, but he was either unable or unwilling to listen. Jenny's frustration spilled over to anger and later silence.

After Andre's abduction, Mike changed even more. His work suffered and a perennial anger took hold of him. In time, that anger turned to deep sorrow, like a hole had opened up into his very soul. Their personal life became calmer but they remained distant. They were two people alone, sharing a house.

Jenny went up the stairs and walked down the short hallway to a bedroom door. She opened it and before her was Andre's room. Her eyes took in all of his personal belongings, including the reinforced windows that kept him from having nocturnal jaunts on the sloped metal roof of the house. To her his essence was still here. She remembered the sweet moments when he would come to her so she would chase him and upon catching him she would tickle him until deep belly laughs erupted, and when he would get his father to hoist him on his shoulders for walks around the neighborhood.

She turned to face a wall in his room. Hanging on it was a framed picture of Andre, Mike, and Jenny standing in front of the iconic Princess Castle at Disney World. They had gone there for Christmas and it was going to become a family tradition, as Andre loved every second he was there. It was one of the few times they felt like a normal family. Her eyes reddened and tears formed. She murmured aloud as she stared at the photo. "My poor baby. I miss you so much."

CHAPTER FOUR
Revelation

Andre moved with small, rapid steps toward the target house. All the houses on the block were either dark or dimly lit. He slipped into an alley next to the building. His eyes gazed at a side window on the second story. This was his designated point of entry.

He maneuvered to a fence that separated the house from its neighbor, climbed to its top, and then grabbed a series of pipes attached to the side of the structure. Andre moved deftly, exerting no strain as he propelled himself upward.

Brooks had moved the Explorer to a busier thoroughfare one street over. He knew that he was within proximity to two interstate systems, and that he could have the vehicle and its cargo heading safely back to home base within seconds of the job being completed. He was careful to park in a manner that would simulate as closely as possible the training Andre underwent for this assignment. Even if the vehicle was not in the precise spot, the boy would still recognize it, but in this case it was positioned perfectly.

Myers fidgeted in his seat, saying nervously, "I can't believe this is happening."

"Just relax, Doc," Brooks retorted. "Look at his vital signs. The kid is scaling the side of a house as we speak and his heart is barely beating."

Andre reached the window. It was locked. This had been expected and planned for. Andre placed his hand in his pouch and took out a long piece of metal that resembled an ice pick. Andre's small hand encased a leather grip at the sharp object's base.

While supporting himself with one hand, he slipped the thin metal between the space where the window and sill met and pushed back the lock. The window opened with a slight creak. After slowly raising the window, Andre slipped through it, emerging into what appeared to be a living room. To his right was the entrance to the kitchen. Along the wall was a stairwell leading to the rear entrance of the house. To his left was a hallway next to a set of stairs leading down to the front door. A bedroom, a bathroom, and another bedroom followed. At the end of the hall was the door he was looking for.

The interior of the house was quiet and dark. Rumblings and other types of sleep sounds could be heard from the two bedrooms. Andre routinely entered occupied homes and apartments. He was accustomed to the sounds he was hearing so he had no problem staying focused on the task at hand. The dark hallway resembled the same passage that he had gone down numerous times before during his simulated training.

Andre slid the pick into his pouch and began advancing, gliding more than walking, silently moving forward. His mind began to form images recalled from the training he had received for this assignment. Everything he was seeing now was in-sync from what he had gone through at the agency training facility. The steps he took down the hall were perfectly matched to the ones he had taken during his simulations.

The door to the room he was looking for was ajar. Andre slipped through the narrow opening, moved to a desk with a computer, and sat down. The computer was identical to the one he had trained on back in Washington. To his left he noticed another door, which joined the last bedroom with this room. To his right on the far wall was a map of the United States. It had pushpins of various colors stuck in it, all marking specific locations. However, it was not the pins that caught Andre's interest.

Andre stood up and made his way slowly to the map. This image was not something he had been prepped for but it was still familiar. With his right index finger, he carefully traced a line down from the top of the map to Louisiana. His finger stopped to a spot north of Lake Pontchartrain. Pulling his finger away, he tilted his head, first left, then right. He repeated the process again this time from the eastern and western sides of the map and finally from the southern side. Each time his finger stopped at the same location as before.

As Brooks gazed at his monitor, he suddenly sat up straight in his seat. A look of alarm crossed his face. Myers, startled by the sudden movement, shifted his gaze towards Brooks. "What's wrong?"

Brooks answered abruptly, "The kid's vitals just went haywire! His pulse rate has spiked dramatically!"

Andre reached up and began pulling all the pins from the map, neatly piling them in his hand. He only left the four corners of the map pinned. He then tore the map from the wall. A loud noise echoed out as the map pulled free, its tacked corners remaining stuck to the wall.

The sound awakened the man sleeping in the next room. Fueled by adrenaline he leapt out of bed and burst through the door to the office. He scanned the room quickly and he immediately noticed the office door leading to the hallway was wide open. His eyes then widened in disbelief. Walking briskly down the hall was a small black silhouette.

The man gave chase, his long black hair and dark countenance steeled with anger at the intruder. He shouted in a foreign tongue as he closed in on the small form directly in front of him. Suddenly, he felt jolts of pain coursing through the soles of his feet. His yells were dotted with curses. His housemate, who had been asleep in the other bedroom, bolted upright as he too awakened to the commotion outside his door.

The man fell back against the wall trying to relieve the pain in his feet. He raised one foot up while angling the other foot on its side, trying to maintain his balance. He found several pins of different colors protruding from his sole. He looked down and saw the floor littered with pins.

Andre reached the top of the stairs and stopped. His pursuer had pulled the pins from the first foot and was now busy working on the second. Andre did not move as his adversary began limping furiously towards him, cursing loudly in a strange language.

Andre stuffed the map in his pouch and with both hands he grasped the top of the banister and elevated his body horizontal to the floor below him. Fluidly he swung both legs together and with surprising force propelled his feet into the attacker's chest and midsection.

The man absorbed the blow and crumpled onto the floor. His breath evacuated his body and he moaned as his sternum cracked loudly. Andre, now on his feet, took one step and grabbed his victim by the hair with his left hand. He raised his head and with his right hand delivered a chop to the man's throat directly on the Adam's apple. The man's eyes widened as he struggled to breathe.

The second man came out into the hall. He saw his comrade lying near the stairs, grasping his throat and chest, apparently unable to speak. No one else was visible and the house was now still.

Brooks was still watching the monitor. Frowning he uttered, "Something has gone wrong. His vitals are those of someone exerting energy and he should have been back by now!" Brooks grabbed what appeared to be a small communication device and stuck it in his ear. With his right index finger pressing on it, he pushed a button and spoke, "I need a position on the Rat and I need it now!"

Brooks' monitor blinked. On it were Andre's coordinates, including a map. "He is on the next street right in front of the house!" Brooks exclaimed. He started the ignition and peeled the car from its parked position. The SUV's tires squealed as he turned right onto the cross street in front of him. He then made a sharp turn back to where Andre's coordinates indicated he would be.

With the Ford Explorer idling, both Brooks and Myers peered carefully for any sign of the boy. Brooks cut the lights and pulled directly in front of the targeted house. Lights were on upstairs. The front door of the house was open. "The signal says he should be right here," Brooks stated flatly. What was unusual was that Andre's vital signs were no longer registering.

Against his better judgment, Brooks got out of the SUV, pulling his sidearm from his holster as he exited the vehicle. Carefully he kept his eyes on the open front door of the house. As he stepped onto the sidewalk, he felt a crunch under his foot. Still eyeing the door, he reached down and picked up a black glove. It was Andre's monitoring device, its hardware crushed by Brooks' weight as he stepped on it. Also on the ground was the flash drive.

Brooks hurriedly returned to the SUV, his face white and sullen. He started the ignition and drove away. Myers began to speak, but was silenced as a raised hand, palm open jutted towards him. Brooks then pressed his index finger against his earpiece. He took a deep breath. "We have a big problem. The Rat is out the cage! I repeat: the Rat is out the cage!"

CHAPTER FIVE
The Hunt Begins

Wilson was sunken into his desk chair. He stared at the clock on his desk, cracking his knuckles repeatedly. His brow was furrowed. Too much time had passed. At that moment, his cell rang. He grabbed it and placed the device to his ear. Wilson listened intently as the night's events were unfolded to him. He twisted and swiveled nervously in his chair as he processed the information. He passed the words over in his mind, the code for disaster that he hoped he would never hear. "The Rat is out the cage."

Wilson was speaking directly with the field office in Naperville, Illinois. The botched operation had taken place in Forest Park, a township north of Chicago. He had four additional operatives he could send out immediately. Brooks and Myers were still combing the vicinity.

Wilson's voice was steady as he relayed instructions to his agents. "Listen carefully. Get everybody over there in two separate vehicles. Form a perimeter around the targeted area. It will be daylight soon so he should be easy to spot. I mean, he is a child dressed entirely in black. He also has no idea where he is and he can't read or talk. Move fast, as we have to get him before some pillar of the community gets civic-minded and tries to bring him to a police station."

Wilson placed his cell down. He tried to imagine what had triggered Andre's actions. More disturbing was that Andre had known what the monitoring device was, as he immediately had removed it. That indicated that his leaving the house was not out of fear or disorientation but rather was a conscious decision. It also meant that he might try to evade his keepers. They had tried installing a microchip under his skin but Andre would dig it out, with no regard to pain at all. Putting the tracker in the glove was a solution to that problem. A bad choice in hindsight.

Wilson pondered the events that had just transpired. His prodigy had, of his own accord, abandoned his assignment, and was at large in an area that was on the outskirts of the third largest city in the nation. The thought of Andre exercising free will had never been anticipated or planned for. As such, there was no protocol in place from which to give his men instructions. Wilson was flying blind.

Wilson picked up the mobile phone again, punching in the numbers deliberately. A groggy Coleman Tate answered the phone, mumbling a barely coherent hello. The response was firm. "This is David Wilson. We need to talk."

Tate was the head of Homeland Security. He was diminutive at five feet five inches tall, and possessed many of the traits associated with a Napoleonic complex. It was his idea to retain Wilson's division under the new administration, and it was he who had signed off on the Andre Waters project. The one condition was that he had to be personally informed by Wilson on the results of every one of Andre's missions. Wilson did not want to make this call, but knew if he didn't that Tate would certainly call him for a report.

Irked from being awakened at the early hour, Tate listened as Wilson briefed him on Andre. Tate reported directly to the President. The President was not aware of Andre Waters or the existence of David Wilson's rogue agency. As such, Tate would be held responsible if this incident became public. The President was halfway into his second term but the re-election had been a narrow one. This pattern of events, if discovered by the press, would taint the President and his administration. Impeachment was a very real possibility.

Tate was agitated. "Dave, this is serious shit. I mean, you say this kid can't talk or read but yet he shed his tracking device? What if he can talk?

He could take us all down. He knows all our locations and movements. He has been on over a dozen missions. You have to find him!"

Wilson paused on the other end. He couldn't discount what Tate was saying, but he was skeptical as to the level of risk Tate alluded to. Wilson knew how long it had taken just to toilet train Andre. He remembered the daily regimen of repetitive tasks required just get Andre this far. It amounted to four years of training that included twelve-hour days, seven days a week, plus an additional year just on Andre's specific assignments. He woke up at the same time, ate at the same time, and went to bed at the same time every single day. He had to train for a solid month just to be able to complete a mission that might last a few minutes. In all that time the boy had never uttered a single word.

Tate continued, "This kid has combat training, doesn't he? He might be approached by a Joe on the street and put him in the hospital, or worse!"

Wilson interrupted, "Andre has never eliminated a subject. He is trained to subdue and run. If anything, he will avoid contact with people. My guess is that he is holed up somewhere within a block of his last assignment. Believe me, Cole. We'll find him. I have my whole team looking for him."

Tate responded firmly. "David, I understand you are taking all the appropriate steps but you know our agreement. If anything with this project ever went wrong, you knew there were no second chances. It is always zero room for error. This project has to be shut down and this kid has to be found. Once he is, you know what you have to do."

"Cole, you know I will do my duty, but do you understand that Andre cannot compromise our situation? He can't talk. I mean this is my cousin's son. You want me to kill a member of my own family?" Wilson was now flushed and angry but didn't show it in his voice. The comment about his family was bullshit. He wanted Andre alive, but not out of any concern for the child's welfare.

Tate, his voice rising, shouted into the phone, "You lousy son of a bitch! You kidnap the brat not giving a shit about him or his parents and now all of sudden you get soft? You listen and you listen hard! You find that kid and you erase him or I will see to it that you take the whole fall. I will not have either the President or myself damaged by this sequence of events. Your ego invented this nightmare and now you have to live with it. Call me when it's done and I better get a call before the sun rises!"

Wilson sat stunned in his chair, the cellphone still placed against his ear even though Tate was no longer there. He paused and then pressed a single digit on his phone.

Brooks was smoking now. A nervous habit, but this was a tense situation. His phone startled him. He answered, but before he could utter a word, a tirade banged into his eardrum. Finally, he began to speak. "Myers and I have been driving for forty-five minutes. We have been moving up and down the street. It's still dark out here."

Wilson listened intently. He flinched at the mention of Myers' name. He had forgotten about the fact that the doctor was also on the scene. He then spoke deliberately. "I have the rest of the Chicago team coming. You need to do whatever is necessary to secure the situation."

Brooks' face began to harden as he reflected on what he had heard. He had been on most of Andre's missions and the thought of killing this child disgusted him. "Director, you are asking too much of me."

Wilson almost sighed. "I know, but this is coming straight from the top."

Wilson took a deep breath then spoke again, "Just find and detain him. No one is going to harm him if we can get him off the street and figure out what happened. He cannot be found by local authorities first!" Wilson was reeling. The lack of preparation on how to handle this type of situation was putting him in a state of confusion.

Brooks listened but was not relieved. "Forgive me sir, but I'm not sure I believe you!"

Wilson disregarded the insubordinate tone. "Just find Andre. Coordinate with the rest of the team and keep me informed. Anything else I should know?"

"We are still in Forest Park but are in proximity to Oak Park. It's a town situated on the L. If he manages to get on a train he could be anywhere in the Chicago area within a short time, or worse, get picked up by the local law enforcement."

Wilson pondered the information. "I'm not sure he knows what a train is but we can't take any chances. Given the situation, that is as good a direction as any to start with. Have one of the teams patrol the nearest train stops." Wilson was using his computer to look at a street map of Oak Park. "My computer shows a station at Harlem and one at Oak Park. Make sure you have a man stationed at each entrance. Let's get a drone in the air as well."

Wilson began to think hard. There had to be more. Where would Andre go? It would have to be a familiar place. He was used to a routine. His thoughts raced back to Jenny and Mike. "One more thing you need to be cognizant of. He may head for a school or a bank. So do a search for banks and schools in the area and check them out."

Wilson hung up the phone and leaned back in his chair, his hands folded behind his head. "So, Andre, it is now a battle of wits." Shaking his head, he began to realize he was not going to enjoy this game of high stakes hide and seek.

CHAPTER SIX
Sanctuary

Andre was moving briskly. He was putting distance between himself, the target house, and his escorts. Maneuvering up and down various streets, he made sure to weave around streetlights to do his best to remain concealed in the early morning darkness.

The map was still firmly clenched in his hand. He kept glancing at it while his eyes darted about, taking in his surroundings. Images formed in his head. Andre communicated through images. The Picture Enhanced Communications System, better known as PECS, was designed specifically to aid nonverbal mentally challenged individuals. PECS had been part of his training and the result was that Andre absorbed all images and stored them as data. His purpose now was to keep moving until he saw something that was familiar.

As Andre crossed various intersections, he would carefully look up and down both sides of the street. He took in all the details of the structures that he saw, but he never paused or stopped. His vision was clear, aided by the infrared lenses in the mask he was still wearing. He had gotten halfway across one street when a building in the distance caught his eye. He veered left and began moving towards it.

The sight of it triggered a memory from Andre's past. He advanced forward, all the while sorting through his mental catalogue, like a computer retrieving a file. The building was higher in the sky than the one from his memory but the trappings were the same. It had playground equipment and a familiar architectural style. The image in his mind continued to gel with the building he was studying. He referenced the pattern of the windows, the design of the doors, and the various symbols displayed prominently on the façade of the structure.

Andre moved directly in front of it and for the first time since leaving the target house, he was motionless. He peered long and hard at the bricks and mortar in front of him, cocking his head from one side to the other. Then he walked towards it, his black suit becoming one with the night as he slipped into the darkness.

CHAPTER SEVEN
Doris

Doris Plaisance was shuffling around her classroom, happily humming a spiritual she had learned as a child growing up in Garyville, Louisiana. A slight woman with caramel-colored skin, Doris was in her element. Her classroom was her refuge.

Doris had always been bright and practical. She had earned a scholarship to LSU and graduated with a degree in elementary education. She got married, but that union had failed. It wasn't always bad times. The marriage produced a child, a vivacious little boy. He was all Doris could have hoped for. At the age of eight, her son became ill. Cancer had struck her only child and when the disease claimed her baby, it was devastation to the family. The father turned to the bottle and the mother withdrew from the world. The marriage never had a chance.

Turning to her faith, Doris prayed for guidance and understanding. Then fate intervened. An older brother had left Louisiana years earlier and had headed north to find a better future. He had worked for years at O'Hare Airport but had never married. A frugal man, when cancer also claimed his life a will revealed that all of his assets had been left to Doris. This included a house in the village of Oak Park, Illinois, located minutes from Chicago. A bonus was that the house produced income in that it had two apartments. One was on the ground floor with a larger apartment upstairs that her late brother had lived in.

Doris initially contemplated selling the house but then thought that a change of scenery might do her good. So she packed up and moved north, to a new life and a new beginning, away from the pain and sorrow that had previously consumed her. She found a teaching position at St. Edmund's Catholic School. The school was located just a few blocks from her house, and she could walk to all the shops that were clustered in the village. The train was nearby so she had easy access to Chicago and all the amenities that a large city could offer.

Doris was tidying up her classroom. It was Easter break at St. Edmund's. While other teachers were traveling or enjoying family outings, Doris was planning for when her students returned. She wanted to redecorate the walls and have her lesson plans ready.

She had opened a window and a gentle breeze cooled the room. Her second story classroom provided her a view of the trees. The buzz of automobiles passing could be heard. It was early, just after seven o'clock, but Doris never slept in. She figured she would have plenty of time to rest when the Good Lord called her. Suddenly Doris stopped, sensing that she was not alone. The two doors to her classroom were shut and were in plain sight. What was this feeling?

Doris turned slowly and let out a hushed shriek. There, perched in her window, was a small figure covered in black from head to toe. A mask concealed his face but he was staring directly at her. An attached hood was draped over his head. One of his hands had a glove on it.

Doris gathered herself. She recognized that the figure was a child. She also rationalized that if he had meant to harm her he would have done so by now.

Doris moved slowly towards the open window and the solitary figure sitting on its ledge. She smiled softly, as if trying to put the intruder at ease. She began to speak in a soothing voice. "Good gracious child, take that hood and mask off so I can see your face."

The small figure continued to stare at Doris. He was crouched in the window, his back facing a second story drop to the ground. He began to tilt his head from one side to the other. He slowly placed first one foot, and then the other, onto the floor. He pulled his hood back from his head and then slipped his mask off.

Doris gazed at the boy and noticed his angular face, blue eyes, and closely cropped blond hair. She slowly moved towards him and knelt down in front of him. Doris spoke in a hushed tone. "What is your name, baby?"

Andre moved towards Doris. He took her face in his hands. He felt the texture of the skin on her face and then he began to smell her. She reached to touch him and he pulled back. Doris withdrew her hand. "Aw, sweetheart, I won't hurt you. Don't you have a name, a family?"

Slowly Andre stepped forward. He reached in his pouch and produced the torn map of the United States. He had folded it so it was in a neat square showing the entire state of Louisiana surrounded by parts of other southern states. He took Doris by the hand and placed her fingers on a spot just above Lake Pontchartrain.

Doris looked at the map and then at Andre. "What are you trying to show me, honey?"

Andre took the map back and pointed to the same spot he had guided her hand to. He again took Doris by the hand and this time he placed her index finger on the spot north of the lake. Doris looked at her finger on the map but was still perplexed. "Baby, I'm still not sure what you are trying to tell me."

Andre backed away and began flapping his hands and grabbing his ears, moving around the room as if in anguish. He was moaning as if in pain. His frustration appeared to be mounting.

Doris began to put the puzzle together. This child appeared to have autistic tendencies. She had taught higher functioning children with autism back in Louisiana. Most were accompanied by a personal aid assigned to them by the school system. All the ones she had previously met could talk and generally were fixated on specific things. She recalled one child who could tell you everything you wanted to know about automobiles. The make, the model, the miles per gallon, to the size of the engine. They had a tendency to be repetitive to the point of irritation and could become antagonized just from an unusual noise.

Many recoiled from human touch. This child seemed to be more severe, but yet he had some capacity. What was he doing wearing these strange clothes? How did he end up in her window and why was he alone?

"Why baby, that is Louisiana. I'm from there too." She made an effort to keep her voice low, not wanting to cause more distress to the child. "Is that where you are from?"

Andre stopped his erratic behavior and a look of calm appeared on his face. He moved back towards Doris and again pointed to the spot on the map. "Praise Jesus. At least I know what you are trying to tell me now." Doris felt relief come over as she had made a breakthrough with the child.

Andre suddenly grew rigid. His head arched and his nostrils flared, as if he had picked up a scent. He pulled away from Doris and scrambled under her desk.

On the street below, a blue Ford slowly pulled to the curb. Brooks had been in constant radio contact with the four other operatives now in the area. Each had set up a surveillance position on the outskirts of the search area. A drone had also been deployed. Brooks and Myers were to comb the interior. They had been looking for Andre for over three hours and were getting edgy.

Brooks turned to Myers. "The upstairs window is open at that school. We better check it out." Both men exited the vehicle.

Myers turned to face Brooks. "What are we going to do, break down the door? It's obvious there is no school today. It's probably just a janitor letting in the breeze while he cleans up."

Brooks became impatient. "Listen, we can't leave a stone unturned. Wilson said check out the schools and this one has an open window. Just shut up and if we see anybody you let me do the talking."

They approached the door to the school. It was locked. Brooks began to bang on it.

Upstairs Doris was crouched behind her desk. She had been trying to get Andre out from under it when she heard the loud knocking on the downstairs door. "Listen honey, I have to see what that commotion is. I'll be right back, I promise."

Doris left the classroom, walked down the hall, and quickly descended the stairs. The double door at the entrance had the standard push bar that all schools were equipped with to allow for an easy exit if there was an emergency. She moved to the window on the door and saw the two men standing there. They were both wearing suits and appeared to be middle aged. She spoke through the door without opening it. "May I help you?"

Brooks answered. "We are with Child Protective Services. We are looking for a small boy. He is about four foot seven, and is wearing a black leotard. He has mental problems and can't be left unattended."

Doris began to speak but caught herself. There was something odd about these two men. They didn't sound or act like social service workers. The smaller of the two men, the one with glasses and a receding hairline, appeared particularly uneasy. A small bead of sweat had started to work its way down the side of his face and he was not making eye contact with her. She gathered herself and spoke. "I would like to help but would you please be so kind as to produce some identification?"

The hair on Brooks' neck bristled. If this woman had not seen Andre, she would have said as much. The fact that she was asking for ID meant that Andre was here. "Just open the door and I'll show you my credentials."

Doris was now skeptical. "You can show them to me just as well through the window."

Brooks turned to Myers. "Go stand by the car and keep your eye on that window. Yell if anything comes out of it."

As Myers walked away, Brooks returned his attention to Doris. "Okay lady, you win." He reached into his breast pocket and produced his gun, aiming it at Doris through the window. "Open this damn door now before I blow a hole through your fucking face!"

Doris began to shake uncontrollably. She pressed against the bar and the door opened. Brooks took the advantage. He entered and shoved Doris hard, knocking her to the floor. He reached down and grabbed her arm, jerking her upright. "Let's go upstairs!" His tone was angry.

As they ascended the stairs, Brooks kept his gun pointed at Doris. They moved down the hall, Brooks checking the doors and looking through the windows of the classrooms they passed. All locked and all empty and dark.

They had now arrived at Doris' room. The door was open and as they entered Brooks saw the open window. "So I guess you are here all by yourself." He pushed Doris away. His eyes began to peer around the classroom. Slowly he took its measure. He strode to some double doors that revealed a closet with shelving. Hooks lined the wall, a place to hang coats in the winter. The room had no hiding spots and appeared to be empty save for Brooks and Doris. He then affixed his eyes on the large desk at the head of the classroom. Doris, afraid her face would display what she already knew, gazed at the floor.

Slowly Brooks began edging his way towards the desk. He stopped in front of it and lowered his gun so that the barrel was pointing directly at it. He the raised his leg and gave the desk a hard kick. Nothing happened. He carefully moved to the side of the desk. Even the knowledge that he was armed and physically stronger than Andre gave him no comfort. Andre was fast, fearless, and well trained. Brooks had seen Andre incapacitate men his size in combat exercises and he knew he had to proceed with caution.

Brooks gingerly moved behind the desk. With his gun in hand, he crouched and looked. All clear. He then cautiously lowered his head around the side of the desk, even though he knew Andre could not have gone there without Brooks seeing him. Nothing was there. The room was indeed empty. Brooks stood up and walked towards the open window.

Sticking his head out of the window, Brooks called out to Myers, "Did you see anything?"

Myers, standing dutifully in front of the SUV, shook his head from side to side.

Brooks then wheeled about. Placing his gun in his breast pocket, he turned his attention back to Doris. "I'm going to give you some advice. For your own good, you better listen and follow it." Brooks continued to glare at Doris. "This kid we are looking for is very important. This is a matter that is way above your head and going to the police with this will do neither you nor the kid any good. I don't want you to ponder what just happened or wonder about it. I want you to forget about it but not about the kid. I'm going to give you a card with a phone number on it. If you see this kid again, and I know you saw him, you call it and I promise we will make it worth your while. This kid is important but he is also dangerous, so I'm doing this for your own good and the welfare of that boy. If you do anything stupid, the consequences for you will be severe. Do you understand everything I have just told you?"

Doris nodded her head affirmatively. She was scared but somehow she was keeping her composure. Brooks took a blank card out of his shirt pocket, scrawled a number on it, and handed it to Doris. "Remember what I said. Keep this to yourself and call that number if you see the boy." Brooks fired a parting shot. "You do anything stupid, like going to the police, you will be found, and you will be killed. That's a promise." Brooks then stormed out of the classroom.

Brooks emerged back onto the street. He motioned to Myers and they both got into their vehicle. Shaking, Myers tried to light a cigarette. Brooks looked over at him, produced a lighter, and helped Myers. As Myers puffed nervously, Brooks grabbed his cell. "Director, I just investigated a school over here in Oak Park. I definitely think he was there. A teacher was in the building and I had to confront her to gain access. I think she saw him."

Wilson responded with a tone devoid of emotion. "You did fine Brooks. You and Myers stay close and keep an eye on her. Andre might try to follow her home." Wilson then lowered his voice almost to whisper. "How is Myers holding up?"

Brooks glanced at Myers from the corner of his eye. "I don't know. The subject in question could prove to be a liability if this is not resolved soon."

Wilson caught the cryptic answer. "I authorize you to use your judgment in how you wish to handle that particular matter. What about the teacher? Will she talk?"

Brooks responded quickly, "I think I would have to say that I stand on the same answer I gave you on the previous inquiry."

Wilson also didn't hesitate with his response, "Again, use your judgment." He then hung up.

Brooks placed his phone on the console. They were still parked in front of the school. He started the Explorer and drove a block before pulling over again. He adjusted the rear view mirror so he could see the school. He turned to Myers and handed him a twenty-dollar bill. “Go up to that pancake house and get us a couple of hamburgers and some coffee.”

Myers took the money and exited the vehicle. Brooks thought pensively about how potentially in a matter of hours he might have to kill a physician, a teacher, and a disabled child. He closed his eyes as if in pain.

CHAPTER EIGHT
Contemplation

Doris felt like she was going into shock. The encounters with the small boy and the hulking man had left her drained and her mind boggled. Who were those people and what group did they really work for? Why was the boy so important and why was he dressed in those strange clothes? Why was the child carrying a map? Why was he pointing to Louisiana? How did he happen to find her? That man was prepared to shoot her and maybe the child! How did that little boy get out of her classroom without anyone seeing him?

The man had said the child was dangerous yet he appeared gentle and sweet. A woman who trusted her instincts, Doris knew if the child did indeed have some capacity for violence, he meant her no harm. He was looking for help and judging from what she saw from his pursuers he needed some. What should she do next? Call the police?

Doris felt strongly that the large man had been deadly serious when he said that calling the authorities would be folly. They were probably close by watching her, ready to follow in case the child tried to reconnect with her. The first thing she had to do was get out of the building without anyone seeing her. Once she got safely home, she could then sort things out better. Slowly she rose from her desk. Her window would have to stay open. To close it could possibly alert anyone watching that she was about to leave.

Doris made her way out of the classroom but turned right to use the back stairs that led to the playground. As she descended the stairs, she saw where the janitor had chained the doors from the inside. She then went to the cafeteria door. It was locked but inside the cafeteria was a door with emergency handles. The door opened out to the playground as well. She went into the janitor's closet, got his mop, and using the handle she broke the glass to the cafeteria door.

Doris reached in and let herself inside the cafeteria. She made her way to the rear door and exited to the playground. She was out but still in. The playground had no gate, just a large chain link fence surrounding it. Doris would have to scale the fence to make it off the school property. She was grateful that she had worn khakis and tennis shoes.

She climbed the fence more easily than she anticipated but moved carefully as she began her descent. At last, she was on the ground. Now which way to go? She opted to go away from town. Even though she lived near the train, she would rather go out of the way to her home, as she felt her stalkers would probably be situated closer to the village.

Doris walked four blocks down before turning right so she could begin heading to her house on Maple Street. Eventually, while constantly looking at every car for the large man that had threatened her, she finally arrived at her house and went inside. A walk that normally took five minutes had taken thirty but it was well worth it.

Brooks and Myers continued to sit a few blocks from the school. It was now well after eight o'clock in the morning and neither man had seen Doris leave. No police were on the scene so she had at least taken Brooks' warning seriously. Despite that, Brooks was still uneasy. He shifted in his seat and started the car. He made a U-turn and headed back towards the school.

Brooks parked the car and approached the door to the school. When he had exited, he had wedged a rock in the doorsill in case he had to get back in. The rock was just as he left it so he walked in and started up the stairs.

As Brooks approached the classroom, he noticed the door was still open. He looked in and saw the empty room. He rushed down the hall and down the stairs. To his right was the broken window on the cafeteria door. He realized that he had now lost the teacher as well as Andre. He hurried back up the stairs and entered the classroom. He rifled through her desk, looking for a clue to her identity. He found nothing that could identify the teacher. What else could go wrong? How could he have not gotten her name?

Brooks called Wilson. "We lost the teacher. She must have snuck out the back." Brooks' voice was fatigued. "I never got her name. I'm starting to make stupid mistakes!"

Wilson was eerily calm. "Compose yourself Brooks. I'm coming out personally. When you get back to the car, send all the intelligence you have on the teacher to HQ. Include her description, approximate age, and the name of the school. We'll get an ID on her. In the meantime, I need you and Myers to go back to Andre's target and investigate the interior of the house. We need to learn what set him off and it has to be inside of that building."

Brooks was edgy. "Director, the sun is up. Whoever is in that house might be waiting for us. It could get nasty."

"I am aware of the risk involved but Andre has to be found and we are in dire need of clues. It's a chance we have to take."

Brooks heard the resolve in Wilson's voice. "Myers will be absolutely useless to me in this scenario. What do I do with him?"

Wilson smirked. "Just make sure he goes into the house first. We might solve a couple of problems at once."

The Rat

CHAPTER NINE
A Second Chance

Doris opened the gate to her small yard and went up the stairs to her back door. She opened it and emerged into her kitchen. She looked out her side window, which overlooked a playground for a church-run preschool. She then walked down the hall to her bedroom and carefully peeked out her front window. All the parked cars were empty and she saw no suspicious people lurking about.

Doris turned around and headed back to her kitchen. As she entered, she stopped dead in her tracks. There, standing in front of her, was the child. He had entered her house as quietly as a breeze blowing through an open window. He stood motionless before her, a blank look across his face.

She crept slowly towards the boy. As she neared him, she saw that his hands and face were dirty and he smelled badly. The odor was powerful. It was as if he had gotten into a pile of garbage or even worse, sewerage.

"You poor baby, let me get you out of those clothes." Doris led him to the bathroom and began to strip him. He had soiled himself and the suit was naturally clingy. The combination of sweat, urine, and feces made the suit feel like it was molded to his body. She tried to take the map and metal pick from him but he resisted, maintaining a firm grip on both objects.

Now that he was rid of his dirty uniform, Doris realized that he needed something else to wear. "Baby, you wait right here. I'll be right back. I promise." She smiled warmly at him. "Please, honey, wait right here, okay?" The boy looked blankly at her and sat down on the closed toilet seat.

Doris rushed into her bedroom and dug deep into her closet. She never understood why she had kept her son's clothes. It was just a part of him she couldn't be without.

She found the cardboard box and ripped it open. She rummaged and found a pair of khakis, a blue short-sleeve collared boy's golf shirt, underwear, socks, and a pair of tennis shoes. She paused, staring at the clothes momentarily, before gathering the bundle into her arms and rushing back to the bathroom.

As she entered, she found the little boy standing at the back edge of the tub, dodging the hot water that was pouring into it. On the edge of the sink laid the map and the long metal pick.

"Oh, sweetheart, that water is hot." Doris approached the tub and adjusted the flow until the water was warm. She grabbed a washcloth and she soaped the young boy all over. He settled into the warm bath, and stretched out his legs. He began to splash and flail at the water, a slight grin piercing his lips.

After washing his head and ears, Doris emptied the tub and helped him step out of it. She dried him off and applied powder. She then retrieved the clothes she had gotten from her bedroom closet. "These were my son's clothes. His name was Andre."

Suddenly the boy turned and looked at Doris. A broad smile crossed his face. Doris sat back stunned. She stared at the child and spoke softly, "Is your name Andre?" The boy moved towards her and gently wrapped his arms around her. She hugged him back with a suffocating hold, tears streaming down her cheeks. "Oh you sweet baby. There was a reason you found me. Good God Almighty, there was a reason."

Andre Plaisance had been diagnosed with cancer at age eight. A very aggressive cancer. He endured countless bouts of radiation and chemotherapy. Doris watched with anguish as her son lost his hair and so much weight that he resembled a skeleton. Trips to St. Jude's in

Memphis, Tennessee, were frequent. Through it all, the boy exhibited good humor and tremendous courage. The battle lasted two years. In the end, all Doris could do was sob as she held her son in her arms during his final moments.

She was now holding another Andre in her arms. She held him back and looked at him. Waves of long dormant maternal feelings rushed over her. After her Andre had died, Doris had suppressed all those feelings as a way to deal with her grief. But now, as she clutched this young disabled child, all those emotions came flooding back. There was nothing she could do to save her Andre, but now there was another child in need. In need of her.

"I'm not going to let anything happen to you. God has given me a second chance and I'm not going to let anything happen to you. You understand?" Andre stared back with a perplexed look in his eyes. He then turned and picked up the clothes that Doris had brought into the bathroom.

Andre insisted on dressing himself and Doris noticed how he had secured the metal device and the map under his clothing. She led him out of the bathroom, the soiled black suit he had been wearing held at a distance between her two fingers. She tossed it into her washing machine and took him to the kitchen with the intention of letting him pick out something to eat.

He spotted some apples and bananas and grabbed one of each. Holding them in his hand and under his arm, he used his free hand to grasp a box of pancake mix sitting on a shelf. "Pancakes it is," Doris said.

The boy ate slowly and carefully. Doris offered him milk but he pushed it away. She then poured a glass of orange juice, which he also refused. She finally tried a glass of water, which he downed quickly. After refilling the glass, she sat across from him. "I sure wish you could talk, honey. I'm not sure what to do next."

Andre had finished his meal. Reaching inside his shirt, he produced the map. With a deliberate motion, he again pointed to the spot of land located across from the lake.

"Is that where you want to go?" Doris studied the map. Just north of the lake was a town called Mandeville. "Do you live in Mandeville?" Andre's eyes arched, his face conveying a sense of relief. "Okay, honey. We are going to Mandeville."

CHAPTER TEN
Target House

Brooks pulled the Ford directly in front of the target house. There was no time for a discreet approach. They needed to get in and out as quickly and as inconspicuously as possible. This entry was going to be more difficult, as they were going back into a place with potentially armed and dangerous people waiting for them. Complicating things was that this exercise was going to go down in the daylight, in a busy neighborhood, with his partner being a nervous doctor with no training to rely on.

Myers was now on his second pack of cigarettes. He was sweating profusely. It was eight-thirty in the morning. He turned towards Brooks. "What am I going to have to do?" His voice was quivering.

Brooks took a deep breath. He was screwing a silencer onto his sidearm. "Just do exactly what I tell you and it will all be over quick." Brooks unbuckled his seat belt. "Let's go." Brooks' voice was firm. The two men got out of the SUV and started up the sidewalk.

Halfway up the front steps of the house Myers stopped. "I can't do this. I'm a doctor, not some government agent."

Brooks affixed a steely glare at the trembling physician. "Listen: you are in this. If that kid gets away, you are going down with the rest of us. Now let's get this over with." The sun was higher now and the streets and sidewalks were now active with people beginning their morning routines.

The two men were now standing at the front door. Brooks turned and faced Myers. "I want you to ring the doorbell. When someone comes, if they don't open the door immediately tell them you want to speak with the owner about insurance, vacuum cleaners, anything. I'll be next to you, out of their line of sight. When the door begins to open, I'll make my move."

Myers' hand shook as he raised it to ring the doorbell. As the button was pressed it responded with a loud shrill. The pair waited, Myers standing rigidly in front of the glass pane on the door. Brooks, frowning, was standing next to him just out of sight of the door. "Ring it again." Myers complied. There was still no activity from inside the house.

Brooks was now irritated. "Bang on it!" Myers began to knock, softly at first, then louder.

"Shit!" Brooks exclaimed. He raised his gun, now with a silencer affixed to the barrel, and fired one muffled shot into the door handle. He shielded the gun with Myers' profile.

As the door opened, Brooks shoved Myers forward into the foyer. As Myers stumbled in, a shot rang out and he instantly crumpled to the floor, blood pouring from a wound in his head. Brooks aimed and fired, sending Myers' shooter tumbling down the stairs with a response bullet through his brain.

Using his left hand, encased with a glove, Brooks closed the door. He used the same hand to press against the wall and steady himself as he slowly climbed the stairs, gun drawn. He carefully stepped over the corpse slumped in his path. As he reached the top, his head swiveled. He saw no movement and then it caught his eye. A figure reclined in an easy chair, apparently asleep.

He had no shirt on, but was bandaged around the chest and midsection. Brooks also noticed a dark discoloration around the man's throat. A bottle of prescription pain medication was resting on the table next to the chair. "Excellent work, Andre." Brooks said softly to himself. He placed the gun to the man's head and fired once. Before the shot was fired, the injured man's eyes opened and filled with dread.

Brooks now roamed freely throughout the apartment. He found his way to the office at the end of the hall. Nothing appeared out of the ordinary. Brooks then glanced to his right. Four pieces of torn paper remained tacked to a wall. Something had been ripped from there. He ventured closer. It appeared that what had been hanging there was map of North America. On the wall was a piece of Alaska on one side, a piece of Canada on the other, with pieces of Mexico and Florida visible below. Brooks grabbed his cell.

"Director, I'm in the house. One of our internal problems has been solved and I also addressed our issues with the occupants. The computer was never touched but it appears that a map of the U.S. was ripped from the wall. Do you make anything from that?"

Wilson began processing the information. "A map, you say. Wait a minute." Wilson, who was now on a private jet, sat upright in his chair. The map, finding the teacher, it all made sense. "Andre is trying to go home! Look, I'm in the air and will be at our field house within forty-five minutes. I have a make on the teacher. Her name is Doris Plaisance and she lives at 510 Maple Street in Oak Park. I'm sending the rest of the team to converge on the house. You should be able to get there first, but if he is there don't try to take him alone. Wait until the others arrive. Don't harm him. Just contain him until I can get there."

Brooks was perplexed. "Director, are you sure you want everyone there? Suppose he is not with her?"

Wilson laughed. "If he's not there he will arrive at some point. I guarantee it. Just don't move on him alone. Wait for the others." He wanted Andre alive despite Coleman Tate's orders. He didn't want Brooks to attempt to apprehend him alone and have something go wrong that could inadvertently cause Andre's demise. Even more likely was that Andre might defeat Brooks, and set back their efforts to capture him.

Brooks' tone grew more serious. "Director, I have three dead bodies here. How do I address that?"

Wilson paused briefly. Problems continued to mount. "I don't give a shit about those two terrorists. Just leave them there. I'm assuming the other body is the doctor and you will have to get him out."

Brooks became agitated. "It's daylight! You want me to haul out a dead body in front of a busy street? Damn!"

Wilson was nonplussed. "Wrap him in a sheet. Pop the hatch ahead of time, wait until it's clear, and just throw him in there. Is the vehicle close by?"

Brooks glanced out the window. The blue Ford was in front of the house. It couldn't possibly have moved but somehow it was comforting to make sure. "Yeah, it's right there. I'll handle it." Brooks then clicked off the device.

Brooks got lucky. The first closet he opened had sheets. He grabbed two of them and made his way to Myers' lifeless body. He then wrapped the dead man hurriedly. He stared out the window, then stepped out the door and looked one way and then the other. No pedestrian activity and no cars. The once busy street had become quiet. Brooks exhaled. Maybe he could pull this off after all.

Using the keyless remote, he popped the hatch of the Explorer open. He opened the front door and with great effort hoisted Myers' body onto his shoulder.

Brooks emerged and began the descent of the small set of stairs that led to street level. As he moved down, he struggled with the shifting weight. Suddenly the body fell forward and slipped from his grasp, tumbling onto the sidewalk.

Brooks was aghast! Both of Myers' feet and one of his hands were protruding from the now blood-soaked sheets that surrounded him.

Brooks quickly gathered himself and lifted Myers from the sidewalk while simultaneously flinging him into the SUV. He then slammed the hatch and quickly got in. He started the engine, tires squealing as he roared down the street towards the house of the teacher and hopefully the elusive Andre Waters, leaving the front door to the target house open. "This is truly a day from Hell!" Brooks muttered as he clenched the steering wheel with both hands.

As the vehicle sped away, a frail hand released its hold from the curtain shielding her as she peered out of her window from her house across the street.

CHAPTER ELEVEN
Confrontation

Doris was packing an overnight bag. She tried to use a suitcase but Andre would not let her. She gathered up her belongings but as she zipped the bag shut, she felt a hand reach around and cup her mouth. Andre then turned Doris around, grabbed her by both shoulders, and made a tight lip face at her. He led her by the hand into to the kitchen.

Andre pushed Doris against the wall. He held her there with his hands and gave her a long gaze, as if mentally issuing a command. Doris began to speak but then she paused. She felt strongly that Andre sensed something and she decided not to do anything that might further agitate him. As Andre stared at her, he jutted his lower jaw out, creating the look of a ferocious under bite. Doris closed her mouth and remained still.

Brooks, still anxious from his efforts associated with securing Myers' body, had pulled up in front of 510 Maple Street, a brownstone almost identical in design to the target house he just left. Brooks sat in the Explorer, gathering himself. He then got out and walked up the stairs to the front door. He had decided to disobey his orders. He tried to open the door but it was locked. He took out his gun, the silencer still affixed to the barrel. As he had done at the target house, he fired a silent shot into a door lock. Brooks was the epitome of frustration. He began talking to himself. "I have been on more missions with this kid than anybody. What a load of crap that we need five people to apprehend him."

Brooks started up the stairs. As he reached the top, he saw Andre standing in the living room. Dressed in khakis, a golf shirt, and tennis shoes he resembled any normal ten year old. "Hey, Blondie. It's me, your old buddy Brooks."

Andre stood completely still, his face deadpan, his arms folded behind his back.

Doris, upon hearing footsteps on the stairs, had moved silently to the entryway of her kitchen. She peered around and emitted an inaudible gasp as she saw the man that had threatened her life standing across from Andre.

Brooks, standing at the top of the stairs, looked intently at Andre. With his right arm at his side, gun in hand, Brooks calmly said, "Buddy, I hate to do this but I have no choice. I promise you it won't hurt that bad." Brooks moved into the living room. He slowly raised his gun and began to aim. He was going to shoot Andre in the leg and let a surgeon sort it out.

Before Brooks could fire, Andre threw his pick underhand with a motion similar to rolling a bowling ball. The long piece of metal struck Brooks in his gun hand, piercing the skin and lodging close to the bone of one of his knuckles. Brooks, reacting to the sudden intense pain, did not notice that his shot had careened up towards the ceiling.

With swift strides, Andre approached, and then assaulted his hulking foe. He kicked Brooks in the groin. As the large man doubled over, Andre stabbed two fingers deep into his eyes. Brooks yelled like a wounded animal. Andre then climbed the front of Brooks, swinging himself onto the large man's shoulders while clamping his legs around Brooks' neck, his hands grabbing Brooks' hair and ears for support.

Andre reared his body back and raised himself upward, as if riding a bucking horse. Brooks' hands were groping at Andre's legs, which were cutting off his air supply. Brooks was now standing straight up but Andre continued to rock back and forth, each rocking motion allowing Andre to lean further back, all the while squeezing his legs tighter on Brooks' collapsing esophagus.

Brooks, struggling to breathe, thrashed wildly trying to get his young nemesis off his neck. His foot stepped onto a throw rug and it shifted. As the pair began to fall, Andre shifted all his weight against Brooks' neck.

The thud of Brooks' body hitting the floor was accompanied by the sound of the vertebrae in his neck and back cracking in several places. Andre retrieved the pick from the fallen man's hand and moved away from him. Brooks was still conscious but apparently unable to move.

Doris had seen it all, staring in disbelief from around the door. Andre rushed to her and grabbed her hand. Moving with swift controlled steps, he led Doris towards the back door. They walked deliberately down the stairs and out the back of the house.

At that precise moment two sedans, both black, pulled in front of the Plaisance dwelling. Two men each exited the cars and began walking calmly towards the brownstone building. A stoic-faced man led the way. His name was Frank Johnson, but everyone called him Screw. His brown hair was cut high and tight and he packed a solid two hundred pounds onto his five foot nine frame.

Screw Johnson was a war veteran who was well trained in black operations with over twenty years of experience. He had pulled tours in the Middle East and South America. A decorated Marine, he had personally overseen much of Andre Waters' training. He was Wilson's first recruit after he had fallen out of favor with the CIA for exercising what was believed to be unnecessary force during the interrogation of a suspect who later was proven to be innocent.

Screw stopped at the front of the house and peered around the neighborhood. He spotted a blue Ford Explorer. He then ascended the steps and noticed the front door of the house, the door handle badly damaged. "Damn you. Brooks. You were supposed to wait."

Screw turned and faced the other operatives. "It appears that our colleague has chosen to disregard a direct order. Be ready for anything. I don't have to remind any of you that this kid is the real deal."

They gathered near the front door. Just before entering the house, Screw made a sweeping hand motion and two of the agents headed to the rear of the house.

Slowly moving in, Screw was painfully aware of the absence of any noise inside the house. If Brooks had apprehended Andre, there would be some kind of sound coming from the house, at the very least a confirmation call. If he had failed then their quarry was no longer around. Screw pulled his gun as he continued to climb up the stairs.

Upon reaching the top, Screw immediately saw Brooks lying on his back with his eyes opened wide and his mouth contorted in an awkward manner. Screw placed his firearm back in his shoulder holster and retrieved his mobile phone. He punched in the numbers and Wilson answered. "Director, it's Johnson. The Rat is still loose. Brooks is down."

Wilson cringed with anger. "That stupid bastard!" Wilson paused, regaining his composure. "Listen carefully. Andre is assuredly traveling with the woman. They are going to have to find some transportation. We can't use other agencies to help so this is our show. I just touched down in Naperville. Forget the airports. The boy has no identification. I would send two men to the nearest train stops—Harlem and Oak Park. The others I would send to the bus station and the nearest rental car outlet. I also have a drone in the air."

Screw listened intently. He had forgotten about the small drones they used for surveillance. "I copy. What about Brooks?"

Wilson was curt. "Is he dead?"

"Damn near. I think his neck or back is broken."

Wilson responded firmly. "Leave him there. We'll come back and get him, Myers, and their vehicle after we have captured Andre."

Screw was confused. "Is Myers around here?"

Wilson became irritated. "He got shot at the target house! He's in the back of Brooks' vehicle! Now quit asking questions and instruct everybody to have their laptops and phones synced with our drone. It's mapping the whole area. Start looking for that damn kid! I want Andre in custody by the time I arrive at our base!"

Screw ended the call. He turned to the other men, who were now all gathered inside the house. A solemn look covered Johnson's face as he spoke. "We have work to do."

CHAPTER TWELVE
The Journey Begins

Doris and Andre walked with purpose, careful not to attract attention. When they initially left her house, Doris' first reaction was to find help. Andre had other ideas. He was holding her hand and was leading her towards the business district of the village. Doris realized that she was now committed to helping this little boy. She had decided to go to the bank ATM she frequented regularly. The facility was lined with glass and was located across the street from a police station. Perhaps from there she might be able to enlist some help from the local authorities, as police personnel were constantly filing in and out of the station.

Doris could feel her heart pounding. She was still trying to process what she had witnessed at her house minutes earlier. Her capacity to reason had been compromised. She had told Andre that she would take him home, but how was she going to do that? She wanted to go to the police but she couldn't risk the child running away and being left alone to fend for himself against his adversaries. If she was going to get him home, she would need some cash before they could go anywhere.

They were now in the village shopping district. Doris stopped walking and looked at Andre. She pointed to her purse and then in turn pointed at the ATM kiosk that was now directly in sight. Andre seemed to comprehend and allowed her to walk him in that direction.

They arrived at the ATM. The kiosk was enclosed by glass. They entered and Doris reached into a side pocket in her bag and found her check card. She inserted the card and withdrew three hundred dollars in cash.

Andre stood vigilant, arms folded, facing the street. His feet were planted firmly behind the bullet resistant glass that enclosed the ATM machine. His eyes scanned the perimeter of the street like a hawk seeking its prey. Doris was motionless in front of the cash dispenser, the money she had withdrawn clenched tightly in her hand. She was trying to craft a plan. She had concluded that the airports would be watched and the boy had no identification. She was pondering whether to rent a car. The interstates would be crowded and in theory safe. She didn't want to rent a car here. Better to go to Chicago and do it where the vast numbers of people would offer more protection. That meant taking the train, but they were also crowded, and by her thinking, also safe. The Harlem station was just a few blocks away.

As they slowly exited the ATM facility, Doris glanced at the nearby police complex. She was praying that a police officer would appear and that somehow she could raise his attention without alerting Andre.

Doris looked down at Andre. He first looked at the police station and then fixed his gaze back at Doris. His face was steeled with resolve as he pulled her hand, trying to get her to leave with him. As she tried to point towards the police station Andre dropped her hand and began to move away from her, his legs moving quickly even though his upper body appeared rigid. His running gait was additional evidence of a neurological condition associated with autism. Doris quickly gave chase. "Andre please stop running. I'm sorry. I promise I will take you home."

Andre stopped abruptly. He walked cautiously back towards Doris. Taking her hand the pair began moving again. He affixed a look of disdain at Doris, his lower jaw jutting out, as if to warn her not to make them deviate again from the task at hand. To accentuate his ire he thumped his chest with his fist.

Andre's eyes darted about as he walked hand in hand with Doris. They made their way past an array of shops as they continued heading towards Lake Street. They walked until they came to a street that passed under the train tracks that were above them. Directly ahead, a small tunnel appeared.

On the other side was South Boulevard, which would lead them to the Harlem station. Suddenly Andre became rigid and looked towards the sky.

Doris peered up and caught a glimpse of what appeared to be a small toy, remote-controlled plane circling above them. She looked around but saw no one with a control device. It was as if the plane was flying on its own.

Andre looked behind and then from side to side. Doris could tell he was assessing their situation. He locked his eyes on the small plane again. He then looked at Doris with steely intent. He looked up at the plane and then back at her. He looked at the tunnel entrance and back at her. She became frightened. It was apparent that Andre was warning her that there would be more danger.

As they entered the tunnel, Doris tried to resist but Andre shot her a hard look and pulled her forward. As they reached the halfway mark, Andre stopped abruptly. Doris, not seeing anything in front of them, began to speak. Before she could utter a word, a man appeared from the shadows near the other side of the tunnel and stood directly in front of them.

The stranger slowly began walking towards them. "Time's up, kid." Cedric Shaw said in a deep baritone voice. "Just come with me quietly and... well, you know the old saying. Nobody will get hurt." He had coal black skin. At six foot three and a chiseled two-hundred-twenty pounds, Shaw was an imposing figure. Before he joined the agency, Shaw had spent some time in the National Football League. A strong safety, his nickname was the Mortician, because after he hit another player, they were "laid to rest."

In Shaw's hand was a Glock automatic handgun. He had been assigned the Harlem station. Shaw had noticed that the majority of the people going to catch the train had emerged from this very location. It was a direct connection to the heart of the village. When the drone made a positive identification on Andre and the woman, Shaw moved into position to intercept the boy.

Doris clutched Andre to her but he pushed her away. Andre slowly walked towards Shaw, his hand stretched out towards him.

"I knew you were a smart kid. Woman you come over here too." Shaw reached over with his left hand and grasped Andre's right hand. Shaw's right hand still had the gun aimed at the boy.

Andre pulled Shaw's hand down forcefully and slid between his legs, doing a complete split. He thrust his left hand up, palm rigid, into Shaw's testicles.

Shaw let out a groan and fell slightly to his left, hitting the brick wall that lined the interior of the tunnel. A shot from the gun ricocheted off the tunnel wall. Andre rocketed to his feet and was now directly behind Shaw. With both hands, he shoved the stricken man's head hard into the same wall. Upon contact, Shaw began to slowly slide down the side of the wall towards the ground, his left knee bent and his right leg stretched completely out. After Shaw had hit the wall, his grip on his gun had loosened and it had fallen out of the agent's hand, bouncing onto the floor of the tunnel.

Andre jumped into the air and upon his descent slammed his right foot down onto Shaw's exposed right knee. A loud popping sound echoed out of the tunnel as tendons and cartilage tore in unison. Andre followed with a roundhouse kick to the bridge of Shaw's nose, breaking it instantly. Shaw fell over backwards, his body racked with pain so excruciating he couldn't speak, yet alone scream.

Andre looked back at Doris and stepped towards her with his hand extended, beckoning to her. She lurched forward towards him. As the pair stepped over the stricken agent, still writhing in pain, Andre stomped on Shaw's face with his foot, cracking a cheekbone. Shaw let out a muted gasp. Andre then reached down and picked up Shaw's Glock.

Andre and Doris stopped just before exiting the tunnel. Again, Andre's eyes peered skyward. As if on cue, the drone reappeared, hovering at low altitude. With a smooth motion, Andre raised the gun, gripping it with two hands. He fired a single shot and the drone split into pieces and plummeted to the ground. Andre then turned and lobbed the gun back into the tunnel. It hit the ground and slid almost into Shaw's motionless outstretched hand.

Shaw slowly opened his eyes upon hearing the shot and subsequent clatter of his firearm striking the concrete floor of the tunnel. He slowly glanced up, fear now accompanying the pain coursing thru his body.

Shaw could hear the rumbling of a crowd that had responded to the noise of the gun being discharged and the drone crashing to the ground. He then dug into his pants pocket and removed his phone. He pressed a button on the small hand held device. Lying on his back, he rolled to his side, his knee, head, face, and groin all throbbing. He placed the cell near his mouth, spitting out some blood and tooth fragments, and gasped into it, "I'm down and I'm hurt bad. They are heading to the train. Just shoot that damn kid. Just shoot him." He then passed out.

Wilson was now at the Naperville field office. He had all the phones synced. He and his agents heard Shaw's desperate plea. "What are everybody's locations? Does the drone still have a visual on Andre?"

Johnson spoke first. "I'm at a car rental place. Rivera is at the bus station and Roth is at the Oak Park station. Roth is the only one who can get to them in time. One other thing. The drone is no longer transmitting. Andre shot it down. We got a visual on one of the laptops that showed him entering the tunnel and then coming out with Shaw's gun on the other side and then aiming and firing it at the drone."

Wilson was slack-jawed. After a long pause he spoke. "Roth you copy that?"

Dennis Roth responded, "Affirmative. Do you want me to engage them? They will already be on the train. There will be witnesses."

Wilson was firm. "Board the train and observe them. Keep your wireless on and we will track you. We need to take them as a team. Just keep us apprised if anything unusual happens."

"Roger, that. Roth out."

CHAPTER THIRTEEN
The L

Doris and Andre moved swiftly up the stairs to the main platform of the Harlem station. She approached the automated kiosk in the station and with shaky hands purchased the train passes. Doris was now sweating from both exertion and fear. Andre was still on point staring hard at every human being who moved past them. With the passes in hand, they moved through the turnstile. The tension grew as people gathered, waiting for the train to arrive. Andre continued to survey the growing crowd, all the while clutching Doris by the hand.

In the distance, the rumble of the elevated train could be heard as it approached. It slowly pulled to a stop and the automated doors pushed open with a whooshing sound. They boarded the train and sat in the first car in seats near the conductor. Doris was still shaking slightly. What had she gotten herself into? She had watched this child brutally beat two large adult men without so much as breaking a sweat or making a sound. Her first instinct was to leave this boy at the next stop, but in her heart she knew that was not an option. Whatever he was now, the very people he had hurt were the ones who had made him that way. He was just trying to go home and nobody was going to stop him. Doris' fear slowly morphed to admiration for this young boy who was so determined and focused. Her resolve returned.

The train moved swiftly to its next stop. A computerized voice announced it as Oak Park. People began entering the train with very few getting off. Harlem was an end of the line stop so most of the people who had gotten on the train from there were still on board.

Dennis Roth boarded the train. Roth was a slight man. At five foot eight and one hundred and sixty pounds, he was much smaller than Brooks and Shaw. Roth was a cat burglar who had been recruited out of prison. He was actually Andre's back up, should the boy ever become incapacitated. With a receding hairline and glasses, he looked more like an accountant than a government agent.

Roth tried to melt into the crowd that had boarded the train with him. He was intent on not giving away his position to Andre. He had to find a seat that would give him a good vantage point. He had scanned the cars towards the back of train finding them virtually empty. His hunch was that Andre would be seated near a door towards the front of the first car.

Andre continued to observe intently the scores of people boarding the train along with those already seated or standing. Suddenly his back arched and his head cocked slightly to the side, again appearing to smell something rather than seeing or hearing it. Doris looked at Andre and tried to see what was getting his attention. She began looking at the passengers. There was a group of teenage boys wearing vintage sports jerseys. There were some young mothers with their children. A few rows down was a man in a dark suit, black hair neatly combed, sitting alone staring downwards.

Andre stood, pulling Doris up with him. She knew better than to resist or question his motives. One reason being he wouldn't answer her anyway, and the second being that he obviously knew better how to handle these types of situations than she did.

Andre strode down the aisle with Doris right behind him. He stopped next to the man in the business suit and shot a look at him from the corner of his eye. He then began walking again.

Roth knew he had been made. What would be his next move? It was almost as if the kid were taunting him. He knew that if the pair went two cars down he would have to follow them. If he didn't they could get off at any time. Even with other agents converging, he decided he needed to act in case they didn't arrive in time. He grabbed his cell and began to speak. "I am on the train just past the Oak Park station. He made me and is on the move. I'm going for it. You need to get to the next stop fast."

Roth rose and after a few quick steps reached across Doris and grabbed Andre by the shoulder. "Hold it!" he exclaimed.

Doris instinctively shoved Roth back. She then screamed. "Help us! This man is going to hurt my godson!" Doris wasn't sure where she came up with that but she felt it was true, that God had sent Andre to her, and that he was now her godson.

Roth grabbed Doris by the collar and viciously head butted her, sending her careening into a seat near a window. He then grabbed Andre by his hair and twisted him around, placing him in a basket hold. This was a common maneuver to restrain a child having aggressive behavior. Roth's hands and arms were folded around the young boy from behind, restraining his arms in the process. Andre was trained to submit to such a grasp but now he was struggling to free himself. Roth squeezed harder and began to inch his arms up. His intent was to choke Andre until he passed out. Doris had righted herself and was now clawing at Roth's arms, trying to free Andre. She continued to scream.

The group of teenage boys immediately turned upon hearing the cries for help. They saw Roth head butt Doris and then grab Andre.

"Hey dude, leave the sista and the lil' man alone!" yelled one of the boys. He was wearing a White Sox baseball cap on backwards and had on a Bears jersey with the number forty and the name Sayers on the back. Gold chains lined his neck and his hands were balled into fists.

The group of five made their way towards Roth. This was a worst-case scenario. "Back off!" Roth exclaimed. "This is government business!" Roth's arms were now around Andre's neck and the small boy was starting to go limp, his hands suddenly dropping to his side. Doris screamed in anguish. "Andre!!!"

The sight of the pain Doris was in and the young boy being assaulted was too much for the group. Another teen shouted in anger. "Get his ass!"

Roth released Andre and Doris grabbed him before he could hit the floor. Roth reached into his breast pocket of his coat but was overwhelmed by the surging youths. He was beaten to the ground, receiving punches and kicks to every part of his body! The group of young mothers secured their children and screamed in unison.

Doris lifted Andre up, who was somehow remarkably alert. Andre turned slowly, saw the carnage, and calmly grabbed Doris by the hand. He led her to the back of the car to an adjoining exit door that lead to the next passenger car. They kept moving until they were all the way in the back of the train. He then pulled Doris to the floor.

The L pulled to a stop. Screw Johnson and Julio Rivera raced up the stairs to the platform just in time to see several Chicago police officers, accompanied by paramedics, storm the train. The two agents waited what seemed to be an eternity before they saw five young men being taken off the train in hand-cuffs followed by Roth's unconscious and battered body being carried out on a stretcher by the paramedics.

One police officer remained on board, standing in the entrance of the first car. He told everyone on the platform to catch the next train and the doors slammed shut. Screw and Rivera stood helplessly, their faces filled with frustration as the train pulled off. They scanned each window looking for Doris and Andre but did not see them.

The policeman who made the announcement was now working his way to each passenger gathering information and taking statements. The process went quickly as everyone in the first car quickly confirmed what had happened.

He finally made it to the back of the train and quickly zeroed in on Doris and Andre, as they were the only ones on this car. The cop had a ruddy complexion and easy smile. "The folks up front told me I would find you two back here. You both have had quite a morning. I'm Sean O'Hara." He extended his hand to Doris and she shook it.

Doris gathered herself. "Why yes sir we did. I'm taking my little Godson to the city. We are going to the Navy Pier. He is autistic but he enjoys watching the boats and playing on the playground there. He wanted to come and sit back here and that man just up and grabbed him for no reason. He was crazy, saying he was with the government. If those boys hadn't stopped him I don't know what would have happened." Doris was amazed at how quickly she had invented the story. Even more amazing was that Andre sat motionless as the officer had approached. His head and eyes were down, seemingly confident that Doris would not betray him.

O'Hara looked at Doris and Andre with compassion. "Those boys got a little carried away with their heroism but we have them and your assailant in custody and we'll sort it out. All the other passengers have confirmed what happened. I understand you were struck during the attack. Do you need medical attention?"

Doris was feeling some discomfort but nothing that alarmed her. She also knew going to see a doctor now could expose them to more danger. "I'm fine. I lost my balance when he hit me but the impact wasn't that hard." Yet another lie but she had to conclude this interview. She wasn't sure what Andre might do if he became threatened. The last thing she wanted was for him to harm a police officer.

O'Hara scribbled some notes and then looked at Doris. "I still think you should see a doctor. With that said, I'm sorry you and your Godson were put through this. We still may need to visit with you later if additional information is required. Can the boy speak?"

Doris looked at Andre and then back at Officer O'Hara. "No sir. He is low functioning and non-verbal."

O'Hara took that information down as well. "If I could see some identification and get contact information from you we can wrap this up." Doris produced her driver's license and gave O'Hara her phone number. She was relieved that none of this seemed to perturb Andre. Her hope was with the authorities now involved they could find out who was pursuing Andre and as such, she could turn him over to the authorities.

O'Hara handed Doris her license. "Thank you Ms. Plaisance. Enjoy the pier."

The train had pulled to a stop. O'Hara turned to leave and then stopped. He swung back around and looked at Doris. "What is the boy's name?"

Doris felt a cold shiver go down her spine. "Andre," she said in a voice just a hair above a whisper.

O'Hara directed his gaze at Andre. "Bye Andre," he said.

Andre didn't move a muscle or look up. It was as if O'Hara wasn't even there.

The doors opened and O'Hara left. As he departed, Doris realized she could have written him a note. She wasn't sure if Andre would have been able to read it but it would have been an opportunity to elaborate further as it pertained to their situation. She suddenly felt a tight grip around her hand. She looked at Andre. He was staring at her with his lower jaw was sticking out. It was if he had read her mind. She exhaled and leaned back in her seat.

CHAPTER FOURTEEN
Frustration

Screw Johnson contacted Wilson from the Oak Park platform. "Something happened on the train. Roth came out on a stretcher along with five other guys in cuffs. The cops wouldn't let anybody on the train and we didn't see Andre or the woman through any of the windows as the train left."

Wilson pinched the bridge of his nose. The chaos of the situation was jarring his senses. "Okay, we need to regroup. We are going to have to get smart about this. Roth is in custody but they will take him to a hospital first. We need to find out which hospital he is in and retrieve him before they try to question him. Hopefully, his injuries are not so severe that he can't be moved. Has anyone heard from Shaw?"

Screw answered quickly. "Not a word. During his last communication he sounded like he was about to pass out. It's possible he could have been picked up by the locals."

Wilson dropped his head and paused. He then spoke in a remarkably calm tone. "You two need to split up. Send Rivera to find Roth. You go back to where Shaw was last and see if he is still there, which is damn unlikely. If he is gone, call Rivera and have him track Shaw down as well. With any luck, Shaw and Roth are at the same hospital. After that, I want you to go and get Brooks. Once you have him, check with Rivera and get a status update. Park your car and use Brooks' Explorer since

Myers is already in that vehicle."

"Copy, sir." Screw then clicked off the cell.

Wilson was truly astounded. His staff physician was dead. Two alleged terrorists were dead. Three of his agents were out of commission with two possibly in a hospital and another incapacitated and maybe dead himself in a teacher's house in Oak Park. His little Frankenstein was on the loose with a civilian assisting him and he was not sure what to do next. His phone rang. Wilson answered to hear the voice of Coleman Tate on the other end.

"David, what the hell is going on? Please tell me you have taken care of that kid!"

Wilson took a breath. "Cole, so far Andre has maintained the upper hand. He has put down three of my men and is still at large."

Tate exploded. "You mean to tell me that you and your elite group of vitamin enriched supermen can't find and kill an eight-year-old!"

Wilson was angered by the outburst but stayed calm. "He's ten, Cole, but you forget his age is his advantage. My men are well trained, but when they see Andre, they see a little boy. Could you shoot a little boy?"

Tate remained furious. "I could shoot him. You can bet your ass on that!"

Wilson kept his focus. "Look, I'm certain I know where he is heading. He is trying to go back to Louisiana. We went back into the target house and found that he had ripped a map of the United States off a wall. He probably showed it to the teacher and somehow she figured out his intentions and is trying to help him. That is valuable information and I'm sure we will be able to intercept them both once we gather more intelligence."

Tate paused and then gathered himself. "David, you know I can't offer any assistance. No men, no hardware, nothing."

Wilson was undaunted. "I realize that but we have to stay optimistic. We know the teacher's name and I bet she will use a credit card at some point. My tech people will be able to track them. If she rents a car or buys a bus or train ticket, we will find her and the boy. The travel time to south Louisiana is at a minimum fifteen hours with many stops in between no matter what they use for travel. We are still in the game Cole."

"What is the teacher's name?" Tate asked.

"Doris Plaisance," Wilson replied.

Tate became somber. "I know you are down to two men. If the FBI gets wind of this it will be a race to see who gets to that kid first. This has become an issue of national security. You also have some loose ends to tie up. I will attempt to assist from my end by blocking FBI involvement if they get a whiff of this. Let me make myself real clear. I can't do that for long. Do you know the efforts that have been made to fund your operation and hide the paper trail? We all go down if this lasts much longer."

Wilson didn't bother to answer. His frustration was turning into anger. An anger that was making him hate Andre Waters!

CHAPTER FIFTEEN
Discovery

Martha Watkins dialed 911 with a sense of purpose. The retired social worker had lived in Forest Park for over forty years. She had watched with dismay as once well-kept homes had slowly deteriorated and streets that had been filled with the voices of children playing now reverberated with cacophonous noises from car stereos blasting what was supposed to be music. Martha considered it her civic duty to call the police and report what she had seen. A large man had thrown a lifeless body into the back of an SUV. Furthermore, he had carried the body from that house where those foreigners lived. She knew those people were up to no good and now she had proof.

It was approximately forty-five minutes before Martha's doorbell rang. She hit her buzzer and waited. Soon she heard a familiar voice calling out as he ascended the stairs of her brownstone. "Miss Martha, it's Baron."

Officer Baron Hopgood was no stranger to the Watkins household. Martha Watkins was a one-woman neighborhood watch. She averaged about three calls a month to the police, often dialing 911, even when the call was not necessarily an emergency. Baron had first met Martha about a year ago and felt sorry for her. Often he would visit her house after one of her calls and find himself having to spend fifteen or twenty minutes drinking some coffee and eating a cookie with her, all the while assuring her that everything was going to be all right.

Baron's head was shaved and he carried about two hundred and thirty pounds on his stocky frame. Right at six feet tall, he could appear imposing until he smiled. He had a friendly demeanor and was patient with the citizens he was hired to protect and serve. "Hey, Miss Martha!" Baron was wearing a broad smile as he reached the top of the stairs.

"Don't you 'hey' me, Baron!" Martha was angry. "I have been waiting for almost an hour!"

Baron took her rebuke in stride. "Aw, Miss Martha. You knew I was getting here as fast as I could. Now, what is this about a dead body?" Baron was surprised by the call. By far this was the most serious incident Martha had ever reported.

As was their custom, she handed Baron a cup of coffee and then told him what she had seen out the window. She then then extended to Baron a piece of paper with the license number of the SUV she had seen pull away with the body in its rear storage area.

Baron peered down at the numbers. Martha looked sternly at the young police officer. "Call in those numbers. You need to find that vehicle."

Baron picked up the receiver on Martha's landline and dialed. He identified himself and requested that the numbers be run on the police computer. He waited, then grunted, said okay and thanks, and hung up the phone. "Martha, these plate numbers do not match anything we have on file in our system. You have to stop making these 911 calls. You can get in a whole lot of trouble if you keep doing this."

Martha grew livid. "Baron, I didn't make this up! I really saw a man throw a body into the back of an SUV and I know I copied those numbers right! Please, God, at least go investigate the house across the street! Please Baron!"

Baron let out a long sigh. "All right, Miss Martha. I'll go over there and take a look. But when I get back you and I are going to have to come to some type of understanding. Now stop trippin' on me and I'll be right back." Baron went down the stairs and out the front door. Martha rushed to her window to watch.

As he crossed the street, Baron looked pensively at the house. "Damn. I hate disturbing people for no good reason."

He walked up the front steps and noticed the front door was not completely closed. He rang the doorbell. No answer. He then knocked and called out that he was a police officer. There was still no answer. He finally pushed the door open and entered.

Baron's mind was racing and he began to mutter aloud. "Damn. These people just probably left in a hurry and didn't close their door good and here I am walking right into their house with no warrant, no nothing, just because some damn crazy woman and her kooky imagination asked me to."

Baron's first step was awkward as his foot jerked suddenly. Looking down he saw what appeared to be blood. He then began to slowly climb the stairs and quickly spotted a dead body sprawled over several steps, face down with blood splattered on the walls. Baron hurriedly pulled his gun from his holster.

He continued to gingerly move upwards, stepping carefully around the fallen man. At he reached the top he saw the second house occupant, a pool of blood on the floor next to his chair. Baron was aghast. "Sweet Jesus!" He raced down the stairs and rushed to his car. He grabbed the radio and began to request support. Martha Watkins shut her curtains, a smile of satisfaction on her face.

CHAPTER SIXTEEN
The Call

Doris and Andre sat placidly amid the throngs of people, many speaking anxiously about the altercation that had taken place a few stops earlier. Doris noticed that those on the train talking attempted to conceal their conversations, but the furtive glances they shot in Doris and Andre's direction betrayed them. Doris was amazed how quickly social media had spread the news. Fortunately, by the time people started recording the action on their phones, Doris and Andre had already begun moving to the rear cars of the L. That meant that while people on the train were assuming it was Andre who had been attacked, there was no video to confirm it.

Doris desperately wanted to get off the train but she had to wait for a crowded stop, somewhere in the middle of Chicago where the masses of people could offer them protection. She had decided on State and Lake. From there they could make their way to a bus station and get out of town. Doris no longer had the nerve or desire to drive a car, particularly all the way to Louisiana.

Doris looked at her watch. It was now ten-thirty. Andre began to look tired as he leaned against her, his eyes closing then opening, as he fought the urge to sleep. God only knew how long that child had been up. He had been through so much since she met him. It was a miracle that he was awake at all.

The train approached State and Lake, the huge red Chicago Theater sign visible as it pulled to a stop. Doris gently nudged Andre and he awakened, eyes wide, searching the car and its contents. Doris spoke softly. "It's going to be fine, baby. Let's go."

They rose together and stepped off the train. They moved down the stairs and onto the busy street. The nearest Greyhound station was about a mile and a half away on West Harrison Street.

Doris led Andre by the hand as they maneuvered through the dense mass of people. Andre's head was tilted upward, looking with amazement at all the skyscrapers. He seemed to forget all the trauma he had been through since this day had started hours earlier.

The walk took about thirty minutes but they finally arrived at the station. The bus terminal was a beehive of activity. "Perfect," she said in an inaudible voice. This had to be a safe place, at least from those assassins that were after Andre.

Safe was a relative statement. Vagrants mingled with the array of travelers, asking for change and food. Even in the middle of the day, people were asleep on the benches and chairs that filled the terminal.

Doris, Andre's hand still firmly in her grasp, approached the ticket counter."When does the next bus for New Orleans leave?"

The man behind the counter never bothered to look up. He tapped noisily into a computer. "Two hours," he said in a gruff voice.

That was too long. She feared that either the men pursuing them would find them by that time or Andre would inflict punishment on a panhandler who might have the misfortune to approach them. "What is the earliest bus you have leaving that is heading south?"

The cashier raised his head and shot a glance at Doris and then Andre. "A bus is leaving for Memphis in ten minutes."

"Fine, I'll have my brother meet us there and drive us the rest of the way." Doris wasn't sure why she felt she owed that man an explanation but she was worried that without one she would appear suspicious.

"Whatever." The cashier could not have cared less.

Doris realized she only had the cash she had gotten from the ATM earlier that morning. Not wanting to deplete it, she produced her credit card. Then she hesitated. Her card could be tracked. She bought the bus tickets with cash.

With the tickets now purchased, Doris and Andre began walking to go board the bus. On the way she saw a pay phone, akin to seeing a Yeti in this era of cellular and wireless communication. She had a cell phone but was afraid that a call from it could be traced. She approached the pay phone and picked up the receiver.

Doris decided to call collect. She no longer trusted any of her cards. Before she could begin punching in the numbers, Andre jerked the phone from her hand, his lower jaw jutting out defiantly. Doris bent over and looked at him directly in the eyes. "Baby, I need to call a friend. I need help to get you home. Please give me the phone back."

Andre tilted his head from one side to the other. Doris felt like he was gauging if she was telling the truth or not. Slowly he returned the phone to her.

Doris placed the collect call. The phone rang several times. "Pick up, Jerome," she said with a pleading voice.

Jerome Plaisance groggily reached for the phone, knocking an empty gin bottle to the floor. "Yeah," he exhaled into the phone.

A computerized voice requested receipt of a collect call. Doris' voice saying her name was then played.

Jerome sat up straight in bed as if struck by lightning. "Doris, sweet Jesus, is that really you?" There was no answer. Then Jerome realized he had not agreed to accept the call. He spoke into the receiver. "Yeah, I'll take it."

"Jerome, I'm sorry to call you like this, but I'm in trouble." Doris' voice sounded shaky. "Listen, I can't talk long. I need you to meet me at the bus terminal tonight at midnight, no questions asked. Will you do it?"

"Memphis at midnight! Damn woman, what kind of trouble?"

"I can't talk about it now, but I need your help. It's urgent. Will you come?" A long pause followed. "Jerome, are you sober?"

Jerome grew angry upon hearing the question, as if it propelled him back in time when such queries were commonplace. "Sober? Yes, I'm sober! This is all screwed up. I have to be at work in an hour." He was not telling the truth about work, in fact he had not worked steadily in over four months. Doris became overcome with emotion. Her voice cracking she spoke softly. "Jerome, please help me. I have nowhere else to turn."

Jerome melted instantly. He hated it when he made Doris cry when they were married and he had done it again. She began to sob harder. "Jerome you have to be there. Please promise me you will be there."

Jerome was cold sober now. "I promise. Just stop crying. I'll be there. You just hang on."

CHAPTER SEVENTEEN
Chaos

David Wilson's phone beeped. The image on the touch screen was Coleman Tate. "David, I'm on my way to Capitol Hill, so I don't have much time. A local woman reported seeing a man carrying a body from a house in Forest Park, Illinois. The police investigated and found the bodies of the men your guy Brooks killed. They did background checks, got suspicious results, and alerted the FBI. I'm trying to stall them, saying that it's my jurisdiction, but things have now gotten complicated."

Wilson had a stunned look on his face as he stared at his touch screen while Tate continued. "The police in Forest Park put out a metro area alert. Oak Park police found a car that fit the description the woman gave and the plate numbers matched. They searched the house the car was parked in front of and found Brooks inside, paralyzed. They also searched the car and upon opening the trunk, they found Myers. They have Shaw in custody as well. A pedestrian found him unconscious with his gun on the ground inside a tunnel beneath a train overpass near the Harlem station in Oak Park. He was taken to the University of Chicago Medical Center and we know Roth is there as well. Chicago police also have the teacher's name from a statement she gave on the train after the incident. Once her address came up after Brooks' body was found in her home, an APB was issued for her and the boy. You can compound all of this with the fact that the Oak Park police found your little thief's work clothes in the teacher's washing machine."

Wilson muttered a barely audible acknowledgement. Tate wasn't finished. "David, the teacher and the boy boarded a bus to Memphis about an hour ago. We got their pictures from a surveillance camera in the station. I'm trying to restrict this information. The FBI already has it and it won't be long before the local authorities have it too. Where are your remaining two men?"

"I had them going to find Shaw and retrieve Brooks. We were then going to get Roth." Wilson's voice was tinged with shock. Homeland Security had located the teacher, Andre, and his men before he could.

Tate responded. "Pull them back when we hang up. I'm on my way to meet with Charles Wong. I'm going to fill him in on everything so that he can get the President to intervene and stop the FBI from learning too much."

Wilson spoke carefully, "Do you really feel it's necessary to see Wong?

"If you want me to keep the FBI out of the way I don't think I have much of a choice," replied Tate. "I have a plane waiting for you at Midway. You and your men will fly to Carbondale, Illinois. I have arranged for a helicopter. Once you get to Carbondale, you switch to the chopper, which you will use to rendezvous with the bus. You need to intercept that bus and retrieve the boy and the woman."

Wilson remained silent as Tate continued, "David, you need to think clearly now. Your project is over but your career may not be if we can get this situation under control."

Wilson stiffened. "I'm on my way."

As Tate clicked off his mobile, his car pulled to a stop on the Hill. He exited the back seat and began to walk. After a few steps, he leaned over suddenly. His breakfast fell to his feet.

CHAPTER EIGHTEEN
Disclosure

This was not going to be a pleasant meeting and Coleman Tate's gait was that of an inmate walking down the corridor of a maximum-security prison for the very first time. His head was down and his face was sullen. He was plodding more than walking. He wanted to be anywhere else but here. Finally, he reached Charles Wong's office—the office of the National Security Advisor for the President of the United States.

Tate took a seat across from a middle-aged woman of about fifty staring into a computer screen. Without so much as a glance at Tate, she spoke curtly, "The Director will be with you shortly."

Twenty minutes later, a door opened. Charles Wong beckoned with his hand. "Come in, Mr. Tate. We have much to discuss."

Wong was a short, portly man with white hair and thick glasses. He had gained the President's trust by living up to his reputation of being a stickler for detail, a tireless worker, and for personal behavior that was beyond reproach.

Wong was born in Hong Kong and came to America as a teenager. An engineer by degree, Wong earned a fortune in consulting work, repairing broken corporations from behind the scenes. His business acumen was extraordinary and his analytical approach to problems made him a savior in the President's turbulent first four years in office. Wong assisted the administration in multiple areas including the national economy, foreign policy, and judicial appointments. He was by title the U.S. National Security Advisor, but everyone on the Hill knew that Wong was practically running the country now.

What Wong was not was a diplomat. His demeanor was blunt and his remarks at times stinging. He made very few public statements or appearances. A lifelong bachelor, Wong's focus was on two things: the safety of the country and the image of its Commander in Chief.

Tate approached Wong's desk and took a seat in front of it. Wong's office always unnerved Tate because of how spartan it was. No family photos on the desk or paintings on the wall. Just a large grease board mounted on the sidewall nearest Wong's desk where he diagrammed strategies along with numerous flat screens all on various news or financial channels. Tate was further dismayed that Wong appeared to be on the offensive even though it had been Tate who had requested the meeting.

Wong turned his back on Tate and went behind his desk. He leaned back in his chair and folded his hands in front of him, letting them come to rest on his ample midsection. He wasted no time playing his cards.

"I feel it is necessary to go over events that transpired in Illinois earlier this morning. Two men were killed in Forest Park, a township north of Chicago. They were identified as Tarek Mohamed and Ahmed Khamari, both of whom were people of interest to us. As such, they should have been under surveillance by Homeland Security. More intriguing is a series of events that happened later. In nearby Oak Park, local authorities found a dead man in the back of an SUV parked in front of the house of a school teacher named Doris Plaisance. Upon inspection of said home an incapacitated man was found in the living room. The SUV was identified as the same vehicle seen leaving the site of the double homicide in Forest Park. The plates on the car do not show up on any conventional law enforcement data base."

Wong arched his eyes as if to stress the significance of the statement. For additional effect he took that moment to rise from his desk and move to the side of it. He gave the impression that it was less of a discussion and more of an interrogation. Wong placed his right hand on the desk and leaned towards Tate. "Later this morning, Ms. Plaisance and a young boy were involved in a separate incident with a man on an elevated train heading to Chicago. The man apparently tried to take the child from Ms. Plaisance. Some youths traveling on the train intervened and beat the man so severely he was found unconscious and had to be taken to a trauma center. We have another man, also badly beaten and in police custody, who was found unconscious in a tunnel underneath the elevated train tracks that connect Oak Park to Chicago."

Wong paused briefly, as if gathering his thoughts. "All four men have been identified. Their names are Cedric Shaw, Dennis Roth, Edward Brooks, and Dr. Joseph Myers. Brooks, Shaw, and Roth are all former employees of various law enforcement agencies or military units. Dr. Myers, the deceased found in the back of the SUV, was a retired psychiatrist. To cap it all we have a report that Ms. Plaisance bought two bus tickets to Memphis. These events, combined with the lack of information on why they happened and what connection the teacher and the child have with them, has left me with the impression that this is piss poor work by somebody. I'm hoping that these incidents are not the result of covert operations that have gone beyond the scope of Homeland Security's vested authority."

Wong's voice began to rise as he stepped back from the desk. Even though Wong had come to the United States years ago, his words were still conveyed with a thick accent, particularly the phrase "piss poor." "I want to know who Shaw, Roth, Brooks, and Myers were working for. I want to know why two persons of interest are dead and a man is found paralyzed in a woman's home. I want to know why these men were pursuing an elementary school teacher who is traveling with an unidentified child with broken bodies left in their wake. Finally, I want to know why you are impeding the FBI from offering what I believe is much needed assistance."

Tate remained composed. "Charles, we had the persons of interest under surveillance. It was us who killed them. The four men you mentioned all work for us. The woman is not of particular consequence but the child is. We need to get him and get him soon. I don't want the FBI's help as it would only complicate a delicate situation."

Wong's head jerked back as if his face had been slapped. "Did I hear you correctly?"

"Yes, we eliminated the persons of interest and I don't want the FBI involved."

Wong began to grin mockingly. "This is rich. Perhaps you would like to explain those reasons to me so I can relieve the President of his apparently unnecessary anxiety."

Tate began to speak. He told Wong everything. The formation of the agency headed by David Wilson, the abduction and training of Andre Waters, and the scope of Andre's missions right up to the day's events. When Tate finished, Wong continued to stare at him with a deep penetrating glare. Wong had returned to his seat. He swiveled in his chair, placing his back to Wilson, and he ran his right hand through his hair.

Wong turned his chair back around and looked directly at Tate. His scowl was menacing. "I should have you arrested and placed in jail. Your actions have placed an entire country in jeopardy and you have betrayed a President you swore to protect and serve. As to that little boy, a higher court than what is on this earth will judge you and that bastard David Wilson for what you have done to him and his family."

Wong continued speaking, his voice icy. "My first reaction is to have the FBI move in immediately and end this turmoil, but by doing so I risk exposing the President. As such, I will leave you to continue with your current course of action. I am going to apprise the President of everything. The decision ultimately must be his. You may leave now."

Tate got up to leave. Wong had a parting shot. "You don't so much as fart without letting me know when and where."

CHAPTER NINETEEN
Bad News

Wong had entered the Oval Office to apprise President Odean Brigsby of his conversation with Coleman Tate. Brigsby was a conservative Republican from Mississippi with a lineage steeped in old money. He had attended three colleges before earning a degree and had drifted in and out of various business ventures before entering politics. A former Governor, his campaigns had been fueled by money supplied by special interest groups and family friends.

Brigsby had never been associated with having a keen intellect but he did possess brutish charm. A football player in college at Ole Miss, he was still physically imposing, although he now had a visible gut and thinning hair. Brigsby's brain trust was a cadre of handpicked associates who collectively formed policies and gave him his scripts to read. Brigsby always had some of his entourage with him at all times. He had made fewer overseas visits for summits and meetings than any other preceding President had, and he never met with a fellow world leader alone. His meeting with Wong was not to get his opinion, but to merely find out what action plans were being scripted to address the situation in Illinois.

Wong meticulously filled in the President about the Andre Waters situation. The process was not new as Brigsby needed to be spoon fed information in order to ensure comprehension. Upon the conclusion of his report, Wong sat back in his chair and folded his hands in his lap. He knew what was coming next.

The President looked dumbfounded. He stared blankly at Wong. Without warning, his eyes widened. Apparently, he now understood the severity of the situation. He lurched upward, grabbed a paperweight from his desk, and threw it across the room. He then moved from behind his desk and began ranting, his arms flailing about similar to a spoiled child having a temper tantrum. This was typical behavior when Brigsby received bad news. His diatribes generally contained combinations of profanity laced with questions of how all of this would affect him. There was no concern exhibited for Andre or Doris whatsoever.

Wong always let the President spew without interruption, in much the same way a parent would let a child cry until it exhausted itself. Eventually Brigsby moved back towards his desk and slumped into his chair, swiveling so that Wong only saw his back.

Wong was cool as ice. "Mr. President, I don't want you to stress too much over this. I am confident that the current course of action will rectify this situation before the end of the day."

The President swiveled back around, his face contorted and red. "I don't want to hear any more about this until it is over. I'm going to take a steam."

"As you wish." Wong then got up and left the room.

CHAPTER TWENTY
The Cover Up

After Wong departed the oval office, he began walking briskly. Like a master chess player, he had already made his next move before even seeing the President. As Wong strode down the well-lit corridors, he was still digesting the information Coleman Tate had shared with him earlier. He had a major crisis on his hands.

Wong entered a private office in the West Wing of the White House. Already seated and waiting was FBI director Alfred Dozier. Wong was unusually gracious. "Hello Al. You are looking well."

Dozier smiled slightly, bemused at Wong's demeanor. Normally it was Dozier trying to get a meeting with Wong, not the other way around. Charles Wong was never gracious. He was generally terse and curt with his visitors. Dozier returned the salutation with one of his own. "As are you Charles. I assume you want to be briefed on what is going on in Illinois. We have quite a situation up there. I have spent the better part of this morning going over our action plans with the various bureau divisions in the Midwest. We have crafted a plan to coordinate our interception of the bus carrying the woman and the boy with the state police in Illinois, Missouri, and Kentucky. If you could assist with Homeland Security and get them to back off we can have both of them in custody within the hour."

Wong paused and then spoke. "Al, this is going to be difficult to take but

I have instructions from the President to tell you to cease all operations relating this situation and to inform all the other areas of law enforcement to comply with that order as well. You must also issue a gag order to all involved to give no statements to the media."

Dozier's jaw dropped. "Charles, this is ludicrous. What is the President's rationale for this course of action? Every moment is precious. That bus will make several stops before Memphis. They could get off at any of them."

Wong looked directly into Dozier's eyes. "They won't. We know exactly where they are going and we will catch them. A large coordinated operation such as the one you propose will create national media attention. In that regard, we already have some damage control going on in Chicago as we speak. This is a very delicate situation and you must follow the President's instructions unconditionally."

Dozier was now incensed, and not at the President. He knew who was behind these instructions. "I'm not some shit employee. I'm the Director of the FBI. I have forgotten more about this type of work than Coleman Tate will ever know. This is a travesty!"

Wong remained unmoved by Dozier's outburst. "Al, I have empathy for you right now. I'm feeling compromised as well. Unlike you, I have the advantage of significantly more information, which I'm sorry I can't share with you at this time. I do promise, however, that when this is over I will apprise you fully of all the events that have transpired and I can also assure you that the people in this administration that allowed this to happen will pay a severe price."

Dozier shifted uncomfortably in his seat and began to wipe his glasses. Dozier was an unassuming man, but very bright. He had enormous respect for Charles Wong and sensed that Wong was as frustrated as he was, although he was not showing it.

"Charles I will abide by your wishes, but are you sure we can't assist in some way? There has to be something we can do."

Wong looked away as he responded. "Once we have the woman and child in custody, the Bureau will have plenty to do. I will also ensure that the FBI and its director will receive the vast majority of the credit publicly for their service in resolving this issue."

Dozier sat back in his seat. This had to be an atrocious situation for Wong to barter like this. "What reason shall I offer my people for this course of action?"

"Tell them that Homeland Security is handling the case and that the situation is too sensitive and isolated to risk a coordinated action. You may also tell them that the woman and boy are no threat and that there is no additional risk to the general public. I do want your men to retrieve the bodies of the three who are deceased and provide security for the three that are hospitalized. The men who are alive are not to be questioned. Again, be mindful of a leak to the media."

Dozier arched his eyes. "You will keep me in the loop?"

Wong nodded and spoke. "You have my word." Wong then offered his hand. Dozier took it, gave it a firm shake, then rose from his chair and left the room.

As the door shut behind Dozier, Wong picked up a phone. "I need you to get me Coleman Tate. Make sure the line is secure."

Tate picked up the phone on the first ring. "Cole this is Charles. Al Dozier is calling his men in as we speak. We also are working to pull back the state and local law enforcement as well as controlling information to the media."

Tate exhaled nervously. "How much did you tell Al?"

Wong snorted. "Don't worry, Mr. Tate, he doesn't know about the boy or your agency. I did instruct him to gather up the dead bodies and provide security for your men in the hospital, but they will not be questioned until this is over."

"Charles, I'm sorry I know I'm not in any position to question you on procedure but I was…"

Wong interrupted him in mid-sentence, his voice rising. "You are not in position to question jack shit! Now tell me how you plan to clean up your mess!"

Tate spewed out his answer, having become unnerved by Wong's outburst. "I have David Wilson, Frank Johnson, and Julio Rivera en route. They will intercept the bus and apprehend the woman and the boy."

Wong countered quickly. "How do you propose to do this? Hope they get off at one of the stops?"

"We are going to wait until it gets dark and then use sniper shots from a helicopter to take out some tires on the bus. The passengers will just assume it was a blowout. We plan to do this on an isolated section of the highway. After the bus pulls over, we will move in and retrieve the boy and the woman. We will also take every cell phone on that bus with us as well."

Wong's frowned. "I'm not sure I like this plan. All those passengers being engaged. What if one or more decide to fight back?"

"It is our intent to move quickly. I will say that the passengers would be considered collateral damage if unforeseen circumstances occur. An added precaution is in place in that they are going to use tranquilizer darts in lieu of bullets. We are hoping that no one on board will play hero. The passenger list indicates that the bus is currently only occupied by fifteen people, including the woman and the boy."

Wong frowned. "Cole, I'm almost nauseated listening to this. Why not have men at a designated bus station or just blockade the highway with two vehicles at a specified location? It ought to allow you to extract the boy and woman without using a sniper!

Tate became animated. "You are worried about publicity and so am I. A bus station is public and people will be getting on and off the bus. That so-called child can spot our operatives with ease. I think the little bastard can smell them. If he were to make one of our guys—and he knows all of them—we would have a problem that could potentially be seen by more witnesses than we could ever hope to control."

Tate took a breath and continued. "We can't afford an incident similar to what happened on the train in Chicago earlier today. If that boy sees a blockade, that would alert him. All of those scenarios also allow everyone with a cell phone time to video or take pictures once we are engaged. If we disable the bus from the air in a desolate area, by the time it pulls to the side of the road, we can be on the ground and mount our assault. As stated earlier, everyone on board the bus will just assume it is a flat tire. We can then contain the passengers and capture the kid without anyone recording anything. I strongly believe this plan affords us the best opportunity to manage the situation and have favorable outcome. Once we have them both, we can spin something to the media."

"Just end it." Wong hung up the phone.

CHAPTER TWENTY-ONE
Preparation

The bus was still in Illinois, but the sun was now shining brightly as it was early afternoon. Doris and Andre were sitting all the way in the back by the bathroom. As they had made their way to the rear, Andre had methodically looked at every seat and peered hard at the overhead storage areas. Doris didn't want to sit so close to a place where multiple strangers would be relieving themselves but Andre had insisted.

The odor that emitted each time the door opened and closed only added to the anxiety of the trip for Doris. Andre had used the bathroom once but after he had finished peeing, he remained inside the small enclosure. He examined every corner of the space, touching the walls delicately as if trying to absorb their texture through his fingertips. Andre had kept the door ajar so he could see Doris while he performed his inspection. Doris now knew Andre was memorizing every detail of the bus. She reasoned that Andre had already anticipated ways they could be attacked and was formulating a response to it. Worried about germs she had quickly grabbed Andre by the wrist and thoroughly washed his hands. Even then, he was still studying the layout of the bathroom.

It took Doris awhile to get Andre settled into his seat. He insisted on being on the aisle. Doris concluded that this would allow him to see who got on and off the bus as well as prevent her from getting up without him. After an hour, he began to relax and finally dozed off to sleep. This was calming to Doris as well. She had grown accustomed to his heightened sense of awareness when danger was afoot. The fact that he was now asleep was good. Andre's head was now resting in her lap, and she gently stroked his hair as she leaned her own head against the window.

The slowing of the bus woke both Doris and Andre. He bolted upright and scanned the whole area. He clutched Doris by the hand with grip that was incredibly strong for a child his size and age. People began to move and Andre grew rigid. Doris leaned over and calmly whispered into Andre's ear. "We are just making a stop honey. We will have several of these. Are you hungry?"

The words had their desired effect and Andre relaxed, loosening the grip on her hand. He looked over at Doris and appeared to nod. Again, she spoke in a whisper. "Let's get off and find something to eat." Andre rose from his seat and slowly began moving up the aisle, all the while shifting his eyes from side to side as looked at every person on the bus. When they reached the front, Doris looked at the driver. "How long before we leave again?"

"Fifteen minutes." The driver had pulled out a crossword puzzle book and shot Doris a grin as he spoke.

Andre was standing in the open doorway. He was rigid again, staring at the convenience store that doubled as a bus stop. Doris put her hand on his shoulder. "Let's go, baby. We don't have much time."

They exited the bus and walked past a row of gas pumps. Once inside the store, Andre pointed to a ham sandwich, a bag of pretzels, and a Diet Coke. Doris made the purchases. She got herself some coffee and a honey bun. Sugar and caffeine. She needed to be alert.

They left the store and Doris noticed another pay phone. She lifted the receiver and punched in Jerome's number. She apparently had earned Andre's trust because he offered no protest when she began to make the call. The phone rang repeatedly. When she hung up, she sighed softly. Jerome had a drinking problem, but when he said he would do something, generally he did. The only thing that he ever failed her on was his drinking. The fact that Jerome had not answered the phone gave her hope that he would be there in Memphis waiting for them.

CHAPTER TWENTY-TWO
The Rescue Begins

Jerome Plaisance was putting gas in his car at a filling station located at the intersection of I-10 and I-55 in LaPlace, a town twenty-nine miles west of New Orleans. He had scrounged up enough money for the fuel, food, and drinks. He figured that Doris would pay him back when he saw her. Jerome was wearing a blue tee, jeans, and some scuffed boots. His goatee and hair were closely cropped and his physique was still imposing, with bulging biceps and broad shoulders.

Jerome had worn out his welcome with most of the local trucking companies but occasionally a dispatcher would toss some work his way. He was living at the Uncle Sam's Motel on Airline Highway. The facility offered reasonably priced rooms that were clean, with their own refrigerators, microwaves, and cable television. The motel also had a laundry room and a bar, with all beers going for a dollar. His Toyota Camry was dilapidated. The windshield had spidery cracks and his safety sticker had expired six months ago. The seats were covered with old blankets to hide the tears in the fabric. The car's black finish was fading with white spots dotting the hood and roof.

Jerome still loved Doris. She had been the best thing that had ever happened to him. He remembered her parents' objections to their marriage, that Jerome would never amount to anything. He thought again of his dead son.

Andre was the light of his life, his legacy, his miracle. Jerome never met his father, and he remembered the parade of men that his mother had brought home. None of them were worth a damn and most were abusive. Many times Jerome received a beating himself trying to save his mother from attack. Sometimes he got beaten for no reason other than being in the house.

As Jerome grew older, he became a man to be reckoned with at East St. John High School. Nobody messed with Jerome or you got your ass handed to you. He was the consummate bad boy, the kind you felt excited to be with. His posse was full of sycophants, there for the thrill but also for protection. Girls outwardly protested his overt and graphic advances while on the inside their stomachs fluttered and their knees quaked upon hearing his plans for them. Then he met Doris. She ignored his advances. She made good grades and kept to herself. She never was out at night, as she was always home studying.

Doris was in honors classes but she and Jerome did have one class together—Black History. One day Jerome was called on in class. Before he could utter his standard smart-ass remark, which would usually get him sent to see the principal, Doris whispered the answer to him from behind. Jerome repeated it, saying the name Frederick Douglass.

The teacher, completely astonished, applauded him. It was the first time Jerome had been singled out in a class for something good and he felt elated about it. After class he sought Doris out and thanked her. Then he asked her if she would help him with other subjects. She nodded with a smile and then walked away.

Doris became his tutor and then his girl. Jerome was still a figure of fear and respect in the hallways of the school. But with Doris, he lowered his guard, and they fell in love.

Doris went off to college at LSU and Jerome went to work. They had gotten engaged the night of their senior prom. Doris came home almost every weekend and when she graduated, they got married. A year later, Andre was born. He was such a happy baby. They had bought a small house and fixed it up together. Doris was his rock and Andre his light. Then Andre got sick.

Cancer was something well known in the River Parishes west of New Orleans. Refineries and chemical plants dotted the area and provided jobs. However, the region was also called Cancer Alley and now his son was dying.

Jerome sought solace in a bottle. Soon he began to have issues at work, even some fights. Doris tried to hold things together but when Andre died it became too much. Then one morning Jerome woke up and she was gone. He tried to find her but no one would tell him where she was. He only learned of her new home when the divorce papers were served.

Now, after all these years she needed him. Needed him! Jerome reached into the glovebox of the car and retrieved a pint of vodka. He threw the bottle into a garbage can. He then got into the Toyota and started the ignition. "I'm coming, Baby."

CHAPTER TWENTY-THREE
The Plan Changes

Charles Wong's phone rang. The voice on the other end belonged to Al Dozier.

"Charles, I have updated information for you. The police in Chicago did some serious work while you and I were meeting. They discovered that the woman traveling with the child, Doris Plaisance, is originally from Louisiana and that she had a son who died from cancer at the age of ten. They also deduced that right around the same time she left Louisiana, the Andre Waters kidnapping took place. You might recall the event. That was the little autistic boy whose school bus had been ambushed. It was national news for a few months and the case remains unsolved. The boy was only five or six at the time but he fits the description of the child seen with Plaisance on the L and later at the bus station in Chicago. She even described the boy as being autistic to the cop who took her statement on the train after the scuffle your agent had with those local teens."

Wong felt woozy. He pulled himself together. "What else do you have?"

Dozier continued. "The Chicago police think it's possible that the child she is traveling with and the Waters boy are one and the same, and that maybe she was involved somehow in his original abduction. They even had Louisiana State Police go to see her ex-husband but they could not find him."

Wong placed his left hand on his desk and then spoke deliberately into the receiver cradled in his right hand. "Al, I want to thank you. This information could prove to be invaluable after we intercept the bus. Please continue following orders and I will call you as events unfold."

Wong placed the receiver down. He removed his glasses and rubbed his eyes. He then picked up the phone again and began punching in numbers. Coleman Tate picked up on the first ring.

Tate was silent as Wong relayed the information he had just received minutes earlier. After Wong finished Tate began to speak. "I don't think this changes anything except that it potentially makes this a national shit show if we eliminate the boy and the woman."

Wong grimaced as the words pierced his ears. "I want that boy captured and unharmed. If he can't talk, we can still spin this without doing any additional harm."

Tate was unmoved. "Charles, that still leaves the woman. Someone will have to go down for this if we leave both of them alive." Wong paused a long time before answering. "I already have a person in mind. Leave that part to me." He then hung up the phone.

CHAPTER TWENTY-FOUR
Pursuit

A coal-black helicopter churned through a cloudless sky. Three men sat silently as the rotor blades hummed noisily above them.

The plan was simple. Intercept the bus carrying Andre and Doris soon after the sunset. The best bet for the extraction was a stretch of interstate that ran through rural southeast Missouri. It was as desolate as the road was ever going to get and there was significant open land to set the chopper down while still maintaining tree cover.

The plan had been reviewed thoroughly. Julio Rivera was to shoot out the right rear double tires. This would force the bus to the shoulder of the highway. Screw Johnson would then land the chopper, at which time both Rivera and David Wilson would exit the helo and enter the bus. Wilson would stay in the front of the bus by the driver while Rivera took out Andre and Doris with tranquilizer darts. Screw would still be on the chopper, ready to engage it once the cargo was on board. The engines would be shut down upon landing to minimize any observations from passing cars.

The possibility of civilian interference from the bus passengers was still a factor but since they were going to use tranquilizer darts, at least no one was going to have to die for this mission to be a success. The media would still have to be dealt with, but at least Andre would be apprehended.

It all seemed simple enough, but then nothing today had been simple.

Hours earlier Andre Waters had been on a routine mission, similar in scope to the other assignments he had been on. Yet now they were in hot pursuit of the young boy who so far had outwitted them and in direct confrontation defeated them.

Rivera was gazing out the window. He suddenly let out a guttural laugh. "This kid is like the Rain Man, Rambo, and that kid from Home Alone all rolled together. He even looks like that stupid kid."

Wilson wasn't amused. "I'm hoping you won't be so jovial when we see that bus. That boy is dangerous and he apparently has more on the ball than we thought. You better get your mind right or you'll end up like Brooks, Shaw, and Roth!"

Rivera's smile disappeared. Both Rivera and Wilson were wearing suits. They were rumpled and dusty. Both men were drenched in sweat, not from the heat but from anxiety. They began performing a weapons check. It was the third one they had done since taking off. They then went over the passenger manifest. Fifteen people were on board including Andre and Doris. Twelve of them appeared to be couples. Logically they would be seated together in pairs. With a fifty-five seat capacity, that meant the passengers would probably be spread throughout the bus, which hopefully would make spotting Andre fairly easy.

Screw was tracking the bus and he had to alter his course to avoid overtaking the vehicle in the daylight. He knew that if Andre could hear the helicopter for a prolonged amount of time it would allow him to prepare or possibly exit the bus and thus derail the plan. He had to come up on the bus suddenly if the plan had a chance to work.

Wilson's cell began to vibrate in his coat pocket. He put in ear buds to drown out the chopper's rotors and took the call. After a brief exchange and several head nods, he clicked off the phone and began to speak.

"Listen up. Through a stroke of luck, the Chicago police have this woman as a possible kidnapping suspect for Andre. Turns out she is originally from Louisiana and lost a child to cancer. She left the state around the same time we took Andre, so they linked the two events. Our plan is still a go but we now have a way to cover our tracks with the media.

Rivera asked the obvious. "Then why not turn around and let them handle it?"

Wilson became agitated. "Because I'm not entirely sure the little bastard can't talk! That's why we have to find him first. This is our only shot. If we miss on this then Wong is going to give the FBI the green light. We also have to contain and debrief the woman. She saw a helluva a lot today of what Andre can do!"

The sun had set and cars could be seen below illuminating the road with their headlights as they moved down the now darkened interstate. Screw Johnson's mind began to drift back to his first meeting with Andre.

CHAPTER TWENTY-FIVE
Training Days

Andre had resisted all efforts to learn anything with his first two trainers. His self-abusive behavior had left bruises about his head and face, particularly near his temples and cheeks, all from him punching himself repeatedly. His face would be so swollen that his eyes would be partially closed. Screw was going to be his third trainer and possibly his last. If he wasn't able to get through to Andre, the boy's life was in jeopardy, either from his own behavior, or just the agency killing him outright.

Screw was no dummy. He had graduated from college with a degree in psychology before entering the service. In preparation for his assignment, he had read everything he could get his hands on that was specific to teaching individuals with developmental delays, including autism and other spectrum disorders. One therapy Screw found intriguing was Applied Behavior Analysis. ABA was the most widely recognized protocol to teach individuals with autism and he implemented its core principles into Andre's training. Screw knew the odds were fifty percent that Andre would respond, but he had limited options at this point, as nothing else had worked.

The first few sessions were just an effort to win Andre's trust. Screw wanted to be patient with him and slowly introduce Andre to his training. He also discovered the power of Twix.

One day Screw pulled a Twix from his pocket for himself. Andre suddenly moved towards him and reached for the candy. This was surprising in that the boy had never showed any interest in sweets before. His snack of choice had always been grapes. Screw seized the moment. He made Andre participate in a simple exercise. When Andre complied he was rewarded with the candy. This mirrored the "clicker training" Screw had read about. Individuals with autism who successfully completed a task heard a click and then received a treat. The idea was to ingrain the behavior as a routine.

Screw now had a base to build on, and build he did. Andre over time began to respond, first slowly, and later dramatically. His natural talents emerged like a phoenix from the ashes and before long, he began mastering complex martial arts moves along with gymnastics and other feats of physical fitness. The candy also played a role when Andre began training for specific assignments. It was his standard reward and Screw was always the one to give it to him.

Screw Johnson had become the boy's only friend. It was he who had gotten permission to take Andre on outings in the community. They had visited museums, parks, and Andre's favorite activity, long car rides. Now his job was to hunt him like an animal. Screw fought back his feelings, sympathy, sorrow, remorse, and even love. He reminded himself that he was a soldier and was on a mission. Deep inside he prayed that he would not have to be the one to confront Andre. He shook his head, as if trying wake up from a deep sleep. He focused his eyes on the dark horizon.

CHAPTER TWENTY-SIX
Assault

The darkness of night now shrouded the bus. Some passengers had electronic devices of various sorts to entertain them but most were just looking aimlessly out of windows or trying to sleep. Doris was feeling fatigued and a bit hungry. The pastry and coffee she had eaten had not sustained her. She also worried about Andre and whether he was still hungry. Suddenly he turned rigid!

The helicopter was hovering to the right rear of the bus. Julio Rivera was trying to aim his rifle. With no moonlight to see by, he was relying on his laser sight affixed to his weapon to guide him. He was getting irate. "Damn it, Screw! Hold this bird steady."

Screw Johnson was no less gracious. "Listen shit-head, if you think it's that easy, come take a turn on the stick!"

Finally, a silent shot was sent towards the target, then another. The right rear tires of the massive vehicle exhaled air. The bus rocked violently. Some passengers let out screams as the driver worked to control the behemoth under foot. The bus weaved right and left before the driver got it safely on the shoulder of the highway, his emergency blinkers lighting up the sky.

The passengers on the bus sat transfixed as they watched the helicopter descend from the night sky accompanied by an intense beam of light emitting from its front. It disappeared behind some trees and vegetation that lined the highway. Rivera leapt from the side door of the chopper while Wilson exited from the other side.

Rivera, his face covered with a black ski mask, emerged from the greenery in a dead run. His gun was held in plain sight as he approached the bus and banged on the closed door. When the driver stared back blankly, Rivera pointed the gun in his direction. The door then swiftly opened.

The tranquilizer gun was slightly different from a standard automatic pistol but it looked threatening enough to the people on the bus. Rivera stood at the front and addressed the frightened group. "Everyone shut up and put your head between your knees!" Rivera then scanned the bus. He saw Doris seated in the back.

He moved swiftly down the aisle. Doris was sitting alone, trembling in her seat. "Where did he go?" He was glaring menacingly at Doris.

Rivera then looked to his left at the closed bathroom door. With the gun in his left hand, he carefully grasped the handle and slowly opened the door.

The space was small and poorly lit. Rivera stared at the chemical toilet and sink. He gingerly leaned inside. A sense of anxiety gripped him.

Suddenly Rivera was propelled backwards out of the bathroom. Andre had been wedged up in the ceiling, in plain sight yet obscured by darkness. Rivera was now leaning back against a bus seat, his hands clutching his face. His eyes were searing with pain from the force of two fingers having been plunged into them. Rivera's gun tumbled to the floor as his cries of anguish reverberated throughout the bus. Andre then grabbed Rivera by the shoulders and thrust his knee into the man's groin. Rivera's screams were replaced with a rush of exhaled air as he doubled over while still groping at his eyes with his hands.

Andre picked up the gun and stood over his fallen assailant. Horrified passengers began to yell in in unison.

Wilson was stationed by the front door of the bus and heard the screams. "You get him?" No answer. Wilson yelled again. "Did you get him?"

Wilson drew his sidearm and began to make his way into the bus. Upon entering, he found himself face to face with Andre. He had Rivera's gun pointed directly at him. Wilson then heard a pop, felt a sharp pain in his right leg, and then nothing. Laying in the back of the bus was Rivera, a dart protruding from his neck.

Inside the helicopter Screw was getting antsy. He had turned off the chopper's engines to minimize any problems from highway travelers who might pass the stranded bus and see the tossing of debris from the whirling blades, but he was still far enough from the bus not to hear anything. His view was obstructed by trees. Did they have the kid? Why was it taking so long? Suddenly he looked to his left and saw Doris outside his window looking at him.

Before he could utter a sound, he felt the barrel of a gun pressed to his neck. Andre had entered the helicopter without being seen nor heard. Screw turned his head slightly and saw the boy's blue eyes fixated on him. Doris raised her voice to be heard through the glass that separated her and Screw. "You are going to fly Andre and me out of here." Doris was calm and steady as she delivered her ultimatum.

"Why the hell should I? It's just a dart gun. Tell him to shoot me!"

Doris maintained her nerve. "Are you so sure about that? Are you willing to risk your life on that assumption?"

Screw weighed his options. He knew it was just a tranquilizer gun. The nozzle on his neck gave it away. If the kid shot him, he would be out for several hours. By the time he came to, the woman and Andre could be far away. He knew that his assignment was to apprehend the pair, and now they were about to willingly climb aboard his helicopter. He also had an ace in the hole. He stared at Doris. "Get in."

Screw heard Doris climb into the chopper through the side entrance, which was still open. He glanced back at her. "Secure the door." Doris complied and slammed it shut.

Screw ignited the engine and the blades spun into action, the noise from the motor and gears erupting into the cockpit. Andre dropped the gun and clutched his ears as in agony, his face contorted in pain. The loud noises had disabled him.

Johnson wasted no time. He thrust his right hand onto the stricken boy's throat and began to squeeze! Doris let out a scream and lunged at

Screw. He balled his left hand into a fist and punched her in the face. She recoiled as blood began to pour from her nostrils.

As Screw glared at the helpless boy, still holding his hands to his ears, he saw Andre's eyes pool with tears. The child stared at him in such a way as one would look at a loved one who had betrayed him.

Screw instantly released his grip. He then began pounding the dash of the helicopter with his fists. Andre slumped back in his seat trying to catch his breath, but not once did he remove his hands from his ears.

Screw looked up and killed the engine. He then reached towards Andre and stroked his cheek, wiping away the boy's tears. Andre slowly took his hands from his ears.

Screw looked lovingly at Andre. He spoke almost in a whisper, "I'm so sorry, buddy. I can't believe I hurt you. Don't be afraid."

Doris sat up, wiping her nose. "You know this child?"

Johnson reached under the seat and grabbed some headphones. He gently placed them on Andre's head. "I trained him and now I'm going to get you and him the hell out of here!" Screw restarted the helicopter's engine and they rose up into the dark sky.

CHAPTER TWENTY-SEVEN
A New Plan

Coleman Tate sat by the phone. When it rang, he jerked the receiver to his ear before it could finish. "This is Tate."

"Cole, it's Charles Wong." Wong sounded subdued.

"What can I do for you, Charles?" Tate was not sure he wanted to hear the answer to his question.

"Cole, the plan failed. Missouri State Police picked up two of your men, one of whom appears to fit the description of David Wilson. Both were tranquilized. Passengers on the bus identified the woman and the boy as being the targets, of seeing a helicopter land nearby, and watching the boy take out both of your agents. They also saw the woman and boy disappear into the brush with the helicopter lifting off shortly after that."

Tate sighed. Yet again, Charles Wong had gotten the upper hand on him and he finally had enough. "I give up Charles. What do you suggest?"

"I believe after your young protégé subdued his attackers, he somehow commandeered the helicopter. I am pulling out all the stops. FBI and all local law enforcement. We are meeting with the media and issuing pictures of the teacher and the boy, naming her as a possible kidnapping suspect."

"Commandeered the chopper? How?"

"The boy probably had a weapon on the pilot with the Plaisance woman issuing instructions. I have police all over the main highways. We will certainly get a visual from the ground very soon."

"What happens then?"

"We deal with that after we have them both in custody. Unfortunately, that poor teacher will have to serve as a scapegoat. With luck, she will get acquitted, but her life will be ruined. As for the boy, he will be interrogated." Wong paused then continued. "If he is a security risk, arrangements will have to be made. I do not intend to return him to his parents right away."

Tate gasped. This was a different side of Charles Wong. "What kind of arrangements?"

Wong replied soberly. "I will not have this child harmed, but we may have to perform surgery to ensure his silence. Since he is already disabled, it should be able to be done discreetly. He has been gone for years, so the parents will have nothing to go on."

Wong then focused his attention on Coleman Tate. "Cole, you are through. You, David Wilson, all of your staff, and everyone associated with that bastard agency of yours. The FBI is detaining people for interrogation as we speak. I have people at your headquarters right now shredding documents and cleaning the place. You are to prepare your resignation letter tonight and have it on my desk in the morning. I would cite health reasons for your decision."

"Health reasons? I guess that is as good an excuse as any." Tate's voice had a sarcastic ring to it.

Wong continued. "Wilson and his agent are probably conscious now. I suggest you give Mr. Wilson a call and inform him of everything. A jet is in the air to bring them both back to Washington."

Wong hung up. Tate paused and then began to punch in a series of numbers on his phone.

David Wilson was sitting calmly on the edge of a hospital bed in the emergency room of a hospital the name of which he didn't know. Still reeling from the effects of the tranquilizer, he answered his cell phone. "Yeah," he exhaled into the device.

"David, it's Cole."

"I guess you heard we blew it." Wilson's voice was barely audible.

"I heard. Look I just got off the phone with Wong. I have to resign tomorrow and the FBI is closing you down as we speak. Wong has not only got the FBI involved but also state and local police. They are even going to issue pictures of the woman and Andre to the media."

Wilson, jolted by what he had just heard, barked into the phone. "What is going to happen to me?"

"David, a private jet is on its way to get you and your agent now. I'm not sure what is going to happen next. We probably won't be seeing each other any time soon. Just follow orders and hope for the best."

Tate hung up. Wilson threw the phone across the room and began pulling at his hair. His face reddened as fury welled up inside of him. He was losing! Losing to a mentally disabled child! It was unfathomable!

He rose to his feet and began to pace, trying to calm himself so he could think. He stopped and caught his reflection in a silver pan on a nearby table. His image was distorted and odd. He spoke to it as you would another person, an ominous smile on his face. "A private jet."

CHAPTER TWENTY-EIGHT
Precious Cargo

Screw Johnson was weighing his options. He was rolling scenario after scenario in his head, trying to conceive a plan that would allow him to get Andre and Doris to safety. This whole sequence of events was perplexing. The fact that this unlikely pair that had known each other for less than a day had managed to outmaneuver highly trained government agents and gotten themselves this far required an explanation. There was more to this than he knew and he needed to know the whole story. He looked back at Doris. "I'm just curious. How the hell did the kid get you into all of this?"

Screw flew the helicopter and listened as Doris told the story of the events of the day. She told him about Andre finding her at her school, the map, her encounter with Brooks, how Andre had appeared again in her home, and how she accidentally learned he had the same name as her late son. Andre sat placidly, staring out the window, his ears still shielded by the headphones.

As Doris continued disclosing all encounters she and Andre had endured, Screw began to feel something stir inside of him. It was a combination of regret and sorrow. He was still emotionally hurting from what he had done to Andre earlier, where he had allowed his misguided sense of duty to almost kill the boy. This poor kid was just trying to go home. The government had caged him up against his will and he couldn't even talk or resist what had happened to him until now. He had previously looked at Andre as some sort of government tool. He had led the strike team that had kidnapped Andre off his school bus four years ago. Because of his disability and lack of emotion, he just assumed Andre had no feelings. He never saw him as genuine person. Even when he took him on their field trips, to him it had been no different from walking a dog. Suddenly that was no longer the case. Screw realized that he had chosen his life. While he couldn't just walk away from his profession, he had the comfort of knowing that it had been his decision, not someone else's. This child had battled incredible odds and was being chased by people ready to put him back in a cage, or worse, six feet in the ground.

"Doris, I'm Frank Johnson, but people call me Screw."

Doris sensed a change in his voice. She also was startled that he knew her name. She didn't respond to his introduction.

Screw continued. "If we stay over this highway, the police will spot us from the sky and chase us until we have to land. I have to fly off the beaten path and avoid being seen. It's dark now. If I get into the countryside I think I can make it to the outskirts of Memphis undetected."

Doris became emotional. Until now, she and Andre had been alone. Now this man was asking her to trust him with Andre's and her lives. Tears began to fall from her eyes and she began to speak frantically. "If anything should happen to this baby. I'll die. I'll just die! Tell me why I should believe you?"

Johnson pondered the question. He was amazed, but at the same time not surprised, that this boy had not moved a muscle and was eerily calm even though he had come close to death earlier. He began to speak. "Doris, you have told me about your day. Now let me fill you in on Andre and what you are up against." He began to tell Doris everything about the agency, Andre's abduction, and his missions. He also related to her how, by coincidence, the episodes of her life allowed the FBI to link her to the child and how she would be used as an excuse to divert attention away from the President and his administration. He also stated strongly that he felt that Andre's life was in danger if he were caught, regardless of how he was apprehended.

Screw peered back over his shoulder towards Doris, his own eyes moist from his epiphany. "Doris, this job has required me to do some awful things, things until now I have never regretted. I signed up willingly for this kind of work, and haven't once disobeyed an order. There have been times when I thought what I was doing was wrong but I always told myself it was for a greater good. This time it's different. This is a kid, for Christ's sake. A kid who wasn't given a choice. A few minutes ago I was about to kill him. I think I have an opportunity to do the right thing for once. I'm not going to fail you or him."

Doris dabbed her eyes with a tissue from her bag. "What do you think, Andre?"

Even with his ears covered, Andre seemed to grasp what was going on between Doris and Screw. He touched Screw's face with his left hand. He then leaned over and began to smell Johnson's face. It was as if he was confirming the truth of Johnson's words from the scent of his skin.

"Thanks, Sport." Screw patted Andre's head. Andre reached into Johnson's shirt pocket and began feeling around. He pulled out a Twix candy bar and quickly unwrapped it and began to eat. Johnson grinned. He looked at Andre. "You remembered. Clever boy."

Doris began to smile. "I didn't think he liked candy."

Johnson's grin grew wider. "That's the story on him, but Andre and I know better. He wouldn't take candy from anyone else, ever." Johnson seemed to lose himself for a moment while recalling those times between them. "Let's see what we can do to get off this highway." The helicopter veered right and headed for the countryside.

CHAPTER TWENTY-NINE
Memphis

Screw maneuvered, constantly trying to stay in remote areas to avoid detection. He knew he was racing the clock and a rapidly depleting gas tank. He felt confident he could make it to Memphis but he was worried. He knew that the whole city would be on alert for Andre and Doris. Finding a landing spot in a safe and secure location would be critical.

He kept the craft low, almost at tree level. Every time he changed direction, he informed Doris and Andre of their new heading, assuring them that they were always heading south. Eventually, the Mississippi River was in view, a brightly lit skyline on the horizon.

"Doris, I'm almost on empty." Screw, Andre, and Doris had activated headsets on for communication. "I can get us closer, but I'm going to have to put her down soon. I'm going to see if I can land this bird near the river. From there you two should be able to get into town rather easily. Do you have a plan once we arrive?"

Doris spoke carefully. "I have arranged for transportation. Please forgive me if I don't tell you any more than that."

"Hey, I don't want to know any more. When they find me, they are going to interrogate the hell out of me. The less I know, the better." Screw was laughing as he made his remarks but then his tone changed. "Doris, are you carrying a cell phone?"

Doris nodded. She pulled it out of her purse. The battery life was down to twelve percent but she still had power. Screw held out his hand. "Give it to me."

Doris complied. Screw then cracked his window and tossed both his and Doris' phones out of it. "If they are tracking our phones, and I'm positive they are, this should buy you both some time. When they catch up to me, I'll tell them you threw them out."

They began to dive slightly, hovering much closer to the ground. Screw touched down on the only open spot he could find, the Memphis tourist attraction known as Mud Island. He cut off the engine. The river shimmered nearby.

"This is it guys," Screw announced. "God, I hope you two make it." Screw looked at Andre and then Doris. He began to speak in a deliberate tone. It was obvious that what he was about to say was very important. "You two are going to be on everybody's radar. My guess is that the media will be involved by now. Do your best to get to that bus station in a discreet manner and do not go inside that bus terminal. You and Andre will probably be on every news channel by now. If you are meeting someone with a car, look for them in the parking lot. It will be safer."

Screw raised his right arm and pointed to his bicep. "Andre, shoot me right there."

Doris was stunned. "Shoot you? Good gracious why?"

"I have to cover my ass," Screw admitted. "Do it, Andre!"

Andre stared at Johnson, his eyes soaking in the visage of the man that apparently had been like a father to him in some odd way. Then he fired the dart into Screw's arm. Almost instantly Screw slumped forward, unconscious. Andre let the gun slip from his fingers and it fell to the floor.

Andre and Doris emerged from the dormant helicopter. Andre took a few steps and looked at the river, the outline of the city, and then Doris. Without warning, Andre let out a loud wail. He began to grab at his hair and from there he progressed to beating himself about his ears and head.

Doris was stunned. She rushed to Andre as he threw himself onto the ground, thrashing about as if in agony.

She cradled him and tried to restrain his arms and hands. "My poor baby! What's wrong?"

Andre produced the map, his face stained with tears, pointing repeatedly in frustration at the spot on the map that was home. He continued to cry and moan making a sound that was forlorn and painful.

Doris wrapped her arms around him more tightly as she knelt on the ground next to him. She began to rock back and forth, the moonlight casting its image on the muddy water in the distance.

"Oh, you sweet thing. You thought when we landed you would be home. Oh baby, we are so close. You trust me. We don't have much further to go. We just have to be careful, but I'm going to get you home."

She continued rocking him and stroking his face. Slowly his cries began to subside. They got to their feet. Doris took Andre by the hand and they began to walk. It was late in the evening now. The thought that they both were now fugitives was sinking in. She also realized that this agency Screw Johnson had described knew they were heading to Louisiana. She would have to find Jerome, but how? Did she dare risk walking into the bus station with all the televisions showing their picture? With a cover-up in place, no one would believe all the incredible things Andre had done.

Doris began to cry but wiped the tears away. She had to be strong. All of this was God's will, and He would show her the way. If she could get this boy home to his parents, then at least he would be safe and it wouldn't matter what they did to her. She brushed her hair back with her hand and together they marched forward. Now they just had to find the bus station.

CHAPTER THIRTY
Desperation

Coleman Tate had been seated in Charles Wong's office for over an hour. Next to him was Al Dozier. Wong abruptly strode in and without issuing a greeting, took a seat behind his desk. All the men looked weary. While they were waiting, Tate had briefed Dozier on the extent of Andre's training and the existence of the maverick agency.

Wong spoke. "Al, what is the situation on the missing helicopter?"

Dozier replied softly, "None of the law enforcement situated along Interstates 55 or 59 have reported seeing it. It either landed in a remote area or moved off the main highway. We can establish road blocks, but without knowing the exact location of the boy, or if the helicopter landed, it would not be a smart use of manpower."

Wong nodded. "I believe that perhaps we need to coordinate our efforts on the ultimate destination, which is the area in Louisiana north of that lake near New Orleans. There are only a few ways in. Having a presence there is paramount. In the meantime, the media will be serving us in that it is possible our quarry could be spotted by a civilian, at which time we could pursue those leads." The media Wong spoke of was in full force. Teams of investigative reporters were descending on Chicago and Memphis.

Dozier responded. "That seems prudent. Don't be so sure about the media help. We are already getting reports of alleged sightings. The problem is that they are all over the country. We can't investigate them all."

Wong grimaced. "We can't afford to have a stone unturned. If this boy makes it to his home it will be difficult, if not impossible, to interrogate him and ascertain if he can compromise this government. If he can talk, the President could be impeached. Tate has already lost his job. I have him here strictly to fill you in on what the total situation is. Do you want to be next on the unemployment line? You assisted with the cover up when you agreed to pull your men back in Chicago."

"That's bullshit! I didn't even know about that damn kid and that bastard secret agency until ten minutes ago." Dozier's face was a bright red. He was now standing at the desk, having sent his chair flying backwards as he rose to confront Wong.

Wong sneered at him. "That is your version of the story. You can take your chances with the next administration and the media."

Dozier slammed his fist on Wong's desk. "Charles, you are a damn fraud! You have this reputation of being ethical and beyond reproach, yet here you are covering your fat ass so you can protect a President who can't wipe his own butt!"

Wong was unmoved by the outburst. "Al, I used to be a consultant to private businesses. I saw behaviors in people that shocked me when it looked like they would lose everything. I was hired because invariably I provided solutions that saved their financial skins. My point is that even the best people will resort to desperate measures when placed in desperate situations. Would you agree that this is a desperate situation?"

Dozier remained silent. Wong continued. "The fate of a nation is hanging in the balance. We have occupational forces in the Middle East, the national economy continues to struggle, and we have large pockets of public dissatisfaction with this administration. If that boy can talk, and the President is implicated, we could have both economic and military ramifications. Tate's agency compiled a list of impressive arrests by violating people's civil liberties, even when they didn't warrant such protection." Wong's voice began to rise. "They used a child to do it! I'm not protecting an impotent President. I'm protecting the sanctity of a nation."

Dozier looked up and began to clap in a mocking way. "Bravo, Charles. Bravo. Are we through here?"

"That depends on you. Are we?" Wong was staring hard at Dozier.

"I don't buy all that rhetoric you just spewed but I'm not prepared to go to war with you over this. The Bureau will do its part, as disgusting as that might be." Dozier turned to leave and then stopped. He turned back around and fixed his gaze on Coleman Tate. "Cole, what exactly can this kid do? What should my men expect?"

Tate sat forward in his chair and rubbed his eyes. His voice was almost a murmur. "He was trained to function as a thief. His combat training was strictly worst-case scenario and was based on probability of an encounter. He would react to situations that we simulated. The difference now is throughout all of this he has been making independent decisions and exercising judgment, traits we didn't think he possessed. He has been assessing risk and demonstrating an ability to adapt to random situations. I honestly don't know what you can expect."

Dozier shook his head. "He is a child though. You make him sound like Superman."

Tate slowly looked up. His face was contorted. "This child can run for half a mile without taking a deep breath. He can stay crouched in a ball for hours without moving a muscle, and he knows every place on a human's body that can incapacitate a person with the right blow." Tate's voice began to rise and his face reddened. "This so-called child can scale the side of a two-story building in less than a minute without making a sound! He can run deftly on the edge of a tall building in the wind without losing his balance! He can swim for a mile with relative ease! He has a threshold for pain unlike anyone I have ever seen and he is totally devoid of fear! He's not Superman, but he's damn close!"

Dozier was glassy-eyed. He turned and left the room. As the door closed, Tate focused on Wong. "What now?"

Wong got up from his chair. He walked to a window and looked out of it, lost in his thoughts. "When Wilson arrives back in Washington, he and you, along with all staff related to your agency, will be detained and debriefed. We need to know this boy's weaknesses to aid in his capture.

Tell me, Mr. Tate, does he have any weaknesses?"

Tate pondered the question carefully then responded authoritatively. "He will not deviate from his new mission. He's going home no matter what."

CHAPTER THIRTY-ONE
Revelation

The outside of the Waters household was a circus. Large trucks saddled with satellite equipment were stacked in their circular drive, accompanied by throngs of people, all outfitted with microphones, clamoring for a statement.

Inside the phones were unplugged. Mike Waters tried to handle calls through his cell phone, but even that number had somehow become known to the media. He had drawn all the shades and had placed a large sheet in front of the oblong window that was in their front door.

He and Jenny had learned of the possibility that Andre was possibly still alive the same way the rest of the nation had, from the television set. Jenny had already gotten home when she heard the news. When she called Mike, he had already left work, as his phone had begun ringing off the hook.

Mike had pulled up just as the first news trucks began to arrive. He had raced up the steps onto his porch and bolted through the front door, slamming it behind him.

As the evening progressed, Jenny remained glued to the television, hanging onto every piece of information that unfolded on the story of the fugitive boy and teacher. Mike continued to focus on the mass of people congregated on his lawn.

Soon the media were joined by several St. Tammany Parish patrol cars.

Fred P. Erwin emerged from one of the cars. He positioned deputies at various areas of the Waters house as he mounted the steps. Erwin banged slowly on the door. "Mike, Jenny. It's me, Fred."

Mike opened the door and ushered Erwin in. "Fred, I didn't expect you to come."

Erwin looked compassionately at Mike. "Well, I am the Sheriff. Besides, I wanted to come. You two have been through enough without having to endure all this."

Mike seemed relieved. "Fred, it means a lot to both of us that you are here."

Erwin glanced at the front door. "I'll have that bunch outside dispersed, but it might help things along if one of you would issue some kind of statement. It would give them something to air, and it would make my job a little easier."

Mike sighed. "I can do that. Before we go out, do you have any information that has not been released to the media?"

Erwin looked troubled. "Mike, there is a theory bouncing around but I'm reluctant to say anything because I don't want to alarm you and Jenny."

Jenny turned from the television and faced Erwin. "Tell us what you know."

Erwin looked down at the floor, similar to a child about to confess a trespass. "The thought is that the woman and the boy are heading to Louisiana. We have been told that if we apprehend her and the child, we have to detain them until the FBI arrives."

Mike frowned. "You mean the FBI wants the woman. We will get to see our son immediately, right?"

Erwin grimaced. "No, Mike. They want both of them."

Jenny rose from the couch. "This woman—is it true that she's a school teacher?"

Erwin wrinkled his brow. "As far as I know, yes."

Jenny moved to the other side of the room. She paced nervously as in a type of trance. Slowly her face contorted and tears began to well in her eyes. She then turned her gaze in the direction of her husband.

"Mike, don't you see? He's trying to get home. He must have gotten away from whoever took him and he found a teacher. It makes sense. I used to take him to my classroom. He must have gone to a school, found a teacher, and convinced her take him home."

Mike turned to his wife. "Jenny, this woman may have kidnapped him. Besides, he can't talk. How could he have told her to take him home?"

Jenny grew livid. "Damn it, Mike. Men in black cars took Andre. How could a teacher have caused that? Why is the FBI going to take him away before we can see him? I don't care if he can't talk. Maybe he can by now, maybe he can write, maybe he showed her a map, and—oh my God!"

Jenny fell back against the wall and crumpled to the floor. Mike and Erwin rushed to her. She grabbed Mike by the shoulders. "Mike, I used to show him a map of the United States, and I would point to Louisiana and find Mandeville and I would tell him that was home. Don't you see? He probably saw a map! Please, God!"

Jenny began to sob uncontrollably. Mike was now frustrated and angry—not at Jenny but at his lack of control over the situation. He helped Jenny to the couch. He then looked at Erwin. "Let's do this."

The front door opened and Erwin came out first. "My name is Sheriff Fred Erwin. Mr. Waters will issue a brief statement. He is not going to answer any questions. Once he is finished, all of you must leave and not trespass on their property."

Erwin stepped aside and Mike moved to the front of the porch. "My wife and I are heartened by the fact that our son may be alive. However, we have no real information whether this boy is our Andre. As such, we really have no further comment on the situation. We would appreciate all of you affording us our privacy until this matter resolves itself." Mike then turned and took a step backwards. Erwin then moved to the front of the porch.

"You heard him. Now get it in gear before I tell my deputies to start making arrests."

The media horde began to leave. Erwin and Mike shook hands and Mike went back inside. He saw Jenny back on the couch facing the television.

"Jen, you have to get a grip. We have no control over this. Why don't you try and get some sleep?"

Jenny turned and faced her husband. "Mike, our son is trying to get home and the whole world is trying to stop him. How can I sleep?"

Mike walked over and sat beside his wife. He put his arm around her and pulled her close. "Jen, you know I kind of shut my eyes to all of Andre's problems? I guess I just didn't have the strength to face them fully. Maybe I didn't know him like you did. Do you really think he could be trying to get home now?"

Jenny seemed to brighten. Her face exhibited a slight smile. "Mike, Andre was always independent and in his way a very smart child. You remember how he was when he made up his mind to do something. Yes, I do believe that he is going to keep trying to come home, now that he believes it's possible."

Mike began to smile himself, a smile of pride in his son. "I guess I better make you some coffee. It's going to be a long night. When he does get home we'll need to be ready."

CHAPTER THIRTY-TWO
A Mind Unhinged

The Missouri State police car roared down the highway. It pulled onto a black-top road and headed towards what appeared to be a small airport. Parked in the distance was a private jet, door open and steps lowered.

Standing outside the plane were two FBI agents, Jake Cuccia and Denny LeBlanc. Both were in their late twenties, each with brown wavy hair. They were dressed in dark suits. The car pulled onto the tarmac and sidled up to the resting aircraft. Cuccia approached the car. "We'll take it from here, Officer."

David Wilson stepped out of the patrol car first, followed by Julio Rivera. Wilson stared hard at the two agents with derision. His lips barely moved as he spoke. "Are you two related?"

Cuccia just smiled. "No sir, we are not. Let's go. Director Dozier is eager to speak with both of you. Sir, I will need your phone."

Wilson removed his phone from the inside breast pocket of his suit coat. As he started to hand the phone to Cuccia he suddenly let it drop to the ground. Just as abruptly he raised is right foot and crashed his heel onto the device. Wilson stared at Cuccia with a sardonic smile. "Sorry." he replied. Cuccia looked back at LeBlanc then again at Wilson. He turned sideways and gestured with a sweeping motion towards the aircraft on the tarmac.

Wilson boarded the plane first, followed by Rivera and the two agents. The steps were raised and the door slammed shut. As the plane began to taxi, the patrol car pulled away.

Within moments, the jet was airborne. The jet's cabin had two rear-facing seats and two forward-facing seats. A vacant seat was up front. Wilson and Rivera sat in the two forward facing seats, with the FBI agents seated across from them.

The jet had a single pilot, as Wilson had made it a point to look into the cockpit as he boarded. Normally, a jet required two pilots, but the urgent need to retrieve Wilson and Rivera apparently caused this compromise in protocol.

Wilson had flown on such a jet many times. He knew it had features designed for comfort and efficiency, such as satellite hook-ups for televisions and computers. It also had parachutes. The aircraft was not roomy and the confined space could work to his advantage, particularly if he had the element of surprise on his side.

After about fifteen minutes, Wilson stood up, although he was in a stooped position, as his lanky frame could not become fully erect in the small cabin area. He had to make his move now before the plane traveled too far. LeBlanc, seated across from him looked up. "You need something sir?"

Wilson smiled. "Why yes, I do." Cupped in Wilson's hand was a small pocketknife, its blade exposed. Wilson was mildly amused that a keepsake would now become a lethal weapon, and that he had been allowed to board the aircraft without being searched. People were always underestimating him. Now they would pay for their arrogance.

"I just need to ask if …" Suddenly, without bothering to finish the sentence, Wilson lunged swiftly and shoved the blade into LeBlanc's neck. He pulled it away and then grabbed Cuccia's hair with his left hand. He thrust the knife into his neck as well. Both men grabbed at their respective throats. Wilson stabbed each man again for good measure. Both stab wounds went through the eye. Blood poured out of both men as if a faucet had been opened wide.

He turned and faced Rivera who by now was trying desperately to unbuckle his seat belt, a look of stark terror in his face. As Wilson moved towards him, Rivera raised his arms, his hands open out in front of him. The two men struggled, Wilson trying to stab Rivera, Rivera trying to avoid being gashed, using his outstretched hands to fend off Wilson's swings with the knife. Wilson was fighting like a crazed maniac. His strength fueled by adrenaline, Wilson lunged onto Rivera, who was pressed against the back wall and the window of the plane. Rivera now had both hands on Wilson's wrists, trying to hold off the assault to save his own life.

Wilson head butted Rivera on the bridge of his nose, breaking it instantly. He then bit Rivera on the side of the face, tearing his flesh away. Rivera's grip on Wilson's wrists relaxed and Wilson drove the blade home into Rivera's throat, raking it across the bottom to open a wide sieve. Rivera slumped forward still anchored to his seat, as blood pooled on the floor.

Wilson stood over the body as its life force began to vanish. The aisle was now covered with the blood of all three men. Oddly enough not a drop had touched the killer.

He checked each body, making sure all the men were dead. He lifted a sidearm from LeBlanc's corpse and then moved towards the cockpit.

To the right of the cockpit entrance was a small closet. Inside were parachutes. He took one and placed it against the wall. He could hear the pilot calling out, asking what was going on. The door was shut and the noise of the aircraft's engines had muffled the sounds of the encounters in the passenger area. As a result the pilot was not aware that he was about to meet a maniac.

Wilson twisted the door handle and entered the cockpit. The pilot turned and looked at Wilson. Before he could utter a sound, Wilson placed the loaded gun to his head.

"Listen very carefully. I have no desire to kill you, but I will if I have to. I can fly this plane myself so it's your call. By the way, the bullet will probably lodge in your head so I'm not worried about a window breaking." He couldn't really fly but he was confident the pilot would not doubt his statement.

The pilot remained silent as Wilson continued. "You are to alter your course and head towards Louisiana. There is a small airport in Abita Springs, a town north of Lake Pontchartrain, which is across from New Orleans. You will land, I will get off, then you will be able to leave." Wilson's familiarity with his home state was now serving him very well.

The pilot gained some nerve. "How will I know you won't kill me then?"

Wilson stared at the pilot with a look of a possessed man. "All you need to know is that I will certainly kill you now if you don't do as I have instructed."

The pilot became resigned to his fate. He decided that the longer he could stay alive, the better his odds were. "Okay, that's fine. I'll change course. Just lower the gun."

Wilson disregarded the request. "Just set the course."

The pilot slowly turned the plane. Wilson began to take inventory of the flight panel. He had some ground school training and was vaguely familiar with most of the instrumentation.

For the next two hours, Wilson bragged about himself and how valuable he was to his country. His mind was warping further into a deeper sense of madness.

The monologue was interrupted by the pilot, who informed Wilson that he was descending in preparation of landing. Wilson carefully eyed the instrumentation panel until he saw the button that engaged the plane's auto pilot function. Wilson spoke calmly.

"Get to three thousand feet and level her off so I can scan the terrain. I think we will have to land somewhere else."

The pilot complied. Wilson looked at the panel of gauges and confirmed their altitude. In almost a single motion, he triggered the plane's automatic pilot function and then fired a single shot into the pilot's skull. He shot him in the top of his head so the bullet would travel down into the pilot's body. As such, the plane would retain its cabin pressure. The skull exploded, covering the windshield and side window in blood and skull bits. Miraculously, again Wilson did not so much as get a drop on him.

He moved out of the cockpit and retrieved his parachute. He strapped it on, then opened the emergency door on the side. Within seconds, he had exited the plane, free-falling towards the ground.

As his parachute jerked open, Wilson cast an eye towards the speeding jet. Within an hour or so it would be over the Gulf of Mexico. The parachute was brightly lit by the moonlight. Wilson realized that he was going to be in unfamiliar territory and without transportation. He also realized that he was probably well ahead of that teacher and Andre. Wilson would have to bide some time and needed get to a television. He now would be relying on information, just like everyone else, from the media.

As the ground came up the parachute brushed some trees, but Wilson managed to steer into an open pasture. He landed hard and tumbled on to the ground. Slowly he got up and began the process of gathering up the spent chute.

He placed the wadded up parachute in an unkempt area of high grass. Wilson surveyed the terrain and saw what appeared to be a road off in the distance, barely illuminated by the bright moon glow.

An old oak stood off to the side near two cows standing like silent sentinels. Wilson strolled over and took a seat. He leaned back against the tree and closed his eyes. As sleep began to come over him, his mind remained focused. When he awoke, he was going to find Andre Waters and kill him.

CHAPTER THIRTY-THREE
Strange Territory

Doris and Andre walked slowly through the dark streets of Memphis. She was in a strange city late at night, on foot with a child. The street signs meant nothing and to make matters worse she was quite certain that her picture was being displayed constantly on the various news channels.

Down the street was a brightly lit gas station with a convenience store. A person pulling the graveyard shift might have seen her picture on TV, but she had to find the bus station soon to have any chance of rendezvousing with Jerome, and she couldn't find it without directions.

Doris and Andre approached the convenience store with caution, taking an angle so she could go up the side without crossing the line of pumps. All the pumps were dormant and traffic on the street was extremely light.

She stood on the side of the store and faced Andre. "Baby, I have to go inside that store and get directions to the bus station. You have to stay here and be still. I'll only be gone a second." She began to walk towards the store entrance, shooting glances back at where she had left Andre. She entered the store. Behind the counter a short man, who appeared to be Indian or Pakistani, was working the register. He had a radio on and was glancing at a newspaper.

Doris paused for a second. Could her picture be in that paper? All of this had started this morning so the odds were good that it would not be in the print media until tomorrow. "Excuse me, but I took a cab here to meet a friend and he hasn't shown up. He was supposed to escort me to the bus station. Is it nearby?"

The man barely glanced up. He seemed neither interested in her problem nor her. "Go three blocks down then take a right on Union. You can't miss it. Are you going to buy anything?" His accent was thick but his English was very good.

"Uh, thank you and sure, uh, I'll take some gum, uh, Orbit." She took the gum, paid the man, and walked out the door. What good fortune that they were so close. God was indeed guiding them.

She exited the store and began to walk back to where she had left Andre. As she neared the end of the building, she gasped! Andre was gone! She looked up and down the street, paralyzed with fear. Now what should she do? Suddenly a voice called out to her. "Hey lady. Is this kid with you?"

She wheeled and saw the man holding Andre by the shoulders. In Andre's hands were a bag of pretzels, a Twix, and a Diet Coke. She rushed up to them.

"Lord yes, he's my godson. I told him to wait by the door. He's handicapped and you can see he has quick hands." Doris managed a smile she hoped was convincing.

"You gonna pay for this stuff?" the clerk asked. Doris reached in her purse. "Of course, here's ten dollars and keep the change for your trouble and for giving me directions."

The man took the money and stepped back inside. Doris gathered the food items and opened Andre's soft drink. She then grabbed Andre by the hand and started heading down the street. She was irritated with Andre but rationalized that the child was hungry. She just squeezed his hand and kept walking. They covered the three blocks quickly. As they rounded the corner, visible in the distance was the bus station. Now all she had to do was find Jerome.

CHAPTER THIRTY-FOUR
The Rendezvouz

Jerome Plaisance walked aimlessly inside the bus terminal. He had driven like mad to get to the station in plenty of time. He had gone inside to use the bathroom when his eyes glanced at an overhead television set. There he saw a picture of Doris and another of a young boy whose name was Andre Waters. He listened with shock as the news reported the events in Chicago and Missouri. He heard the speculation that Doris was a kidnapper and that a dragnet was being formed to arrest her.

This woman was not the Doris he knew. She wouldn't harm a fly and was not a kidnapper. So what if the boy had the same first name as his dead son? Doris would never do anything like that. What could he do now?

Jerome's hands were shaking. He hadn't had a drink in hours and this news was not helping his condition. His willpower fading, he began to wonder if a bar was nearby. A drink would settle his nerves and he could think about what to do next.

He walked out of the station and into the parking lot. He found his car and got into it. He began to start his engine when a hand grasped his shoulder from behind. "Hello, Jerome."

Jerome jerked around and saw Doris sitting in his backseat with a white boy.

"Good Lord. Then it's true. You did take that boy!"

Doris sat back. Her worst fears were confirmed. She and Andre were now in the news and every law enforcement agency in the country was looking for them.

"Jerome you know me better than that. Look, just start driving us out of here and I'll explain everything."

Jerome started the car and gave it the gas. As they moved out of the parking lot, Doris began telling Jerome the events that had transpired. By the time they reached I-55, Doris finally stopped talking.

"Damn woman, this is a big damn deal! They is probably gonna put up roadblocks and everything. It won't be long before that guy in the c-store figures out who you and that boy is. Then the shit is really gonna hit the fan."

"Jerome, I don't care. I have to get this child home. If you don't want to get involved, just let us out somewhere safe and we'll find another way."

Jerome began to laugh. "No way, girl. You spent a whole lotta time keeping my ass out of trouble. Now I get to return the favor."

Doris exhaled, as if a heavy load had been lifted. Andre was nonchalant, taking small bites of his pretzel rod.

Jerome spoke again. "Doris, I have a guy in Jackson who owes me a solid. He has a big rig and makes regular runs to New Orleans. We can't use the interstate. They will have that blocked for sure, but if you and that boy is hidden in his rig, he can get us to New Orleans at least."

Doris was nervous. "Jerome, we would have to get over the Causeway from New Orleans and big trucks can't use that. Besides, are you sure you can trust him?"

Jerome laughed again. "I kept that dude from getting killed one night. He knows he owes me and he'll be cool about it. Why don't you two get some sleep? It's going to be a long night. Don't worry about getting across the lake from New Orleans. We'll deal with that when the time comes."

Doris felt weary, but something in Jerome's voice comforted her. "Jerome, I'm so glad you came."

Jerome smiled in the rear view mirror. "Girl, you the only one who never took any shit from me and who genuinely cared about me. Now get some sleep."

Doris angled back on the seat. Andre took the cue and curled up with his head on her lap. Soon they were both asleep.

The car drove into the night leaving Memphis behind. They soon crossed into Mississippi. After about two hours, Doris awakened. "Jerome, where are we?"

"Mississippi. We are about an hour from Jackson. We should arrive at my boy's house at about three in the morning. Holy shit, is he gonna be surprised."

"Jerome, do I know this man?"

"No baby, he's a trucking buddy of mine. After you left me, I got to partying real hard. One night I was in this old joint and Tyrone got up in some man's face over a woman. That man had about fifty pounds on Tyrone and a knife to boot. So I just went over and smoothed things out."

Doris allowed herself a grin. As much as she hated to let on, she loved the fact that Jerome was tough and capable. She could only imagine how he had smoothed things out.

"Anyway, this old boy owes me, and tonight we are gonna collect."

CHAPTER THIRTY-FIVE
Speculation

Al Dozier paced in his office. His phone intercom buzzed. "Director Dozier, its Mr. Wong."

Dozier picked up the receiver. "Yes, Charles."

Wong sounded impatient. "Any news yet?"

Dozier had been dreading this moment. He took a breath and answered. "Charles, the situation has become more complicated. We have no idea where the helicopter is, nor the woman and the boy. However, that is not the worst of it. The plane carrying David Wilson back to D.C. is overdue and cannot be raised by radio."

Wong let out a groan. "What do you mean the plane is missing? How can it be missing?"

"I don't know how to answer that question. My only guess is that Wilson snapped and somehow took the plane over. I have agents heading to Louisiana, specifically the area where the Waters boy is from. We have all the roads in that vicinity under surveillance. It shouldn't be hard as there are few access roads, only state highways and interstates. We have his parents being watched along with agents at airstrips in the towns of Hammond and Abita Springs, as well as the Armstrong and Lakefront airports in New Orleans. Any helicopter or private jet that tries to land at those places will be boarded and searched."

Wong paused for a long time. Finally, he spoke slowly and carefully.

"Al, I applaud your moves. My guess is that neither of those aircraft have our quarry now. Wilson is too smart and the boy has out maneuvered us from the beginning. Don't change a thing, but make sure the parents' house is continuously watched. That is the focal point."

Dozier nodded his head as if Wong could see him. "I agree, Charles. If all else fails, it will end there."

Wong added a caveat. "Al, it is essential that all three are apprehended before they reach the house. If that child makes it all the way home, we have major problems. Your men cannot fail. Keep them in tandem with local law enforcement as well. I had some intelligence run on the parents. The mother is a teacher and respected in the school system and the father is a banker who has been actively involved with numerous civic causes. As such, their whole community is paying close attention to this situation. They are also friends of the local sheriff. If any local law gets to the woman and child first, without an FBI agent, the parents and media could be notified quickly."

Dozier responded firmly. "I understand."

Wong hung up without saying a word.

CHAPTER THIRTY-SIX
Tyrone

Jerome had used mainly old state highways to get to Jackson from Memphis. He, Doris, and Andre were now in the Jackson city limits in a neighborhood of nondescript houses in various stages of upkeep. This area of Jackson was still asleep and the quiet was broken by the noise of the car engine and the various sounds of insects cavorting in the night air.

Jerome pulled into a driveway. As the engine cut off, Doris woke up. Andre remained asleep in her lap. Jerome turned around. "Wait right here, I'll only be a minute." He got out of the car and approached the door. He knocked rapidly. Soon, lights went on in the house. A curtain pulled back and a pair of eyes peeked out. The front door opened revealing a man about five foot seven with a small potbelly and a receding hairline. He smiled broadly, a gap where a front tooth used to be. Jerome entered the house but the door remained open.

Doris waited with Andre in the car for what seemed an eternity. Finally, Jerome came out of the house and approached the car. "It's cool. Let's get inside."

Doris nudged Andre who bolted upright. She remembered the episode he had in Memphis and spoke softly to him. "Baby, we are not home yet. We have to stop for a little while, okay?"

Andre rubbed his eyes, then followed Doris out of the car and inside the house. Upon entering, he scurried past Jerome and the short man and rushed from one room to the other. Finally, he found the bathroom, pulled his pants down, sat on the toilet, and began to pee.

The short man laughed. "That lil' dude pees like a girl."

Jerome grimaced but Doris said nothing. Finally, Jerome made the introductions. "Doris, this is my main man Tyrone Pugh. Tyrone, this is my wife, Doris, and that's Andre on your can."

"Doris, I seen you on the TV. Jerome here says you and that child needs my help. I'm not one to mess with the man, but Jerome saved my ass once so I owe him."

"We appreciate anything you can do Mr. Pugh. We promise not be any trouble." Doris then extended her hand.

Tyrone took it and gave it a firm shake. "It just so happens that I have to make a run in a few hours to New Orleans. I have a van that we will go get the rig in. As I'm loading it, I will sneak you and the boy into my cab. It's not the lap of luxury but New Orleans is only three hours away. After we get there, you three are on your own."

"That is more than generous, Mr. Pugh. I could pay you something for your trouble," Doris said quietly.

"No, no, that's all right. This will make me and Jerome even, right Jerome?"

Jerome nodded his head.

"Okay then. I'm going back to bed for a couple of hours. Y'all make yourself at home. We will leave here at about five-thirty." Tyrone then stretched and began to head back to his bedroom.

Doris spoke up. "What about Jerome?"

Tyrone turned around. "After you and the boy get in the truck, he will follow us in my van. It has Mississippi plates. They may be looking for Jerome and would have his car's license number. Once we get outside New Orleans, I'm going to pull over and sneak both of you into the van. That way if you get caught, I'll just say he stole it." Tyrone let out a cackling laugh and then shuffled off to his room.

Doris, Jerome, and Andre moved to the couch. They turned off the lights and sat in the darkness. Doris turned towards Jerome and whispered softly. "Why do we need to involve this man and what will we do once we get to New Orleans?"

"Doris, that truck will be one of a hundred on the road. Once we get close to New Orleans, we can go over on the Causeway. They don't collect tolls on this side of the lake, and since Katrina there are hundreds more cars crossing that damn thing every day. There is no way they can stop and search all those cars. Traffic would be backed up for miles. I also don't think they will be expecting you and the kid to use the Causeway because of the fact that it is one damn long bridge surrounded by water. If we don't get pulled over, we might get that boy home yet."

Doris began to think about what Jerome had said. The Causeway crossed Lake Pontchartrain and was exactly twenty-four miles long. Surprising to Doris was that she felt that Jerome was thinking soundly about using the bridge. Because of Hurricane Katrina, thousands of people had relocated to the other side of the lake, known commonly as the Northshore, to live on higher ground. The sheer number of cars made searching all the vehicles problematic. Additionally, the bridge itself could be a trap in that it had very few turn around lanes. It seemed logical in an odd way that the authorities would not to expect her and Andre to use it.

"Jerome, are you sure we can trust this man?"

"Baby, if he double crosses us, he knows I'll be able to get to him, even from prison." Jerome then looked at Doris. "What about you, Doris? Are you going to come home after all of this?"

Doris smiled and grabbed Jerome's hand. "I think it's something we can talk about when this is over, assuming I don't end up in jail, too." They both began laughing and Jerome hugged Doris tightly.

CHAPTER THIRTY-SEVEN
A Man Consumed

David Wilson stretched wearily. He saw the sun peeking up over the horizon. He got up, brushed himself off and started to walk to the road. "This is as good a place to start as any," he thought to himself.

He saw a street sign that read Yellow Water Road. Wilson managed a wry smile. The street was dotted with small homes and house trailers. He saw no people and not one car. He began to stroll casually down the soft shoulder, which had deep open-air drainage ditches running along both sides. Eventually, he saw a sign in the distance: Yokem's Reptile Farm. It boasted a collection of snakes, alligators, and turtles. He also saw another road heading east and west directly in front of him. He turned down the gravel drive and walked to a small brick house that appeared to be both a home and the office of the facility. He approached the door and knocked.

The door cracked open. An elderly man peered from around the side. "We ain't open yet. We don't open until ten o'clock. Come back then."

Wilson smiled. "I'm not here to visit, I need a favor. My wife and I were going to a bed and breakfast. We have been having problems lately and I thought getting away would do us some good. Anyway, she picked the place and was driving when we had an argument. She made me get out of the car and I have been wandering around lost. I just wanted to use your phone. I forgot my cell phone in the car."

The old man was unmoved. "You seem mighty dressed up for a car ride.

You just go to that road up there, take a left, and follow it about a mile. You will end up on the service road to the interstate. Turn right and keep walking. You will come to a convenience store. You can use the phone in there."

Wilson smiled broadly. "Thank you, sir, for the information, but I could pay you to use your phone. I'm extremely tired and I would just as soon call a friend to come get me.

The old man grew agitated. "Get the hell off my property or the only car you'll be riding in will belong to the Sheriff!"

Wilson stayed calm. "I'll leave, but could you at least tell me where I am. Like I said, my wife was driving and I wasn't paying attention. It was dark when she put me out."

The man barked at him. "You are in Ponchatoula. Now get off my property!"

Wilson grinned. Ponchatoula was in Tangipahoa Parish, about 20 miles from Mandeville. With a swift motion, he kicked the door, propelling the old man backward. He then entered the room.

Wilson pulled his sidearm and fired a shot into the man's chest. The man's eyes widened in shock as he absorbed the impact. He clutched his shirt and stumbled backward before falling over, blood pooling on the floor around him.

Wilson dragged the lifeless body behind a counter situated to the left of the door. He pulled all the shades and began to scan the room. There on a table behind the counter was a television set. Nearby was a large desk. On top of it was a computer, already on, apparently hooked up to a cable modem.

He seated himself at the desk and began rifling through its drawers. He found some brochures about the reptile farm. He then began typing on the computer, pulling up a map routing website. From one of the brochures, he typed in the address of Yokem's and then the Waters' home address, which he obtained from a white pages search via the internet. Soon, he had directions in hand. He was approximately thirty minutes away by car from the Waters' home.

Wilson then flicked on the television to a national news channel. He was confident his protégé's whereabouts would still be a prominent news item. As the TV came to life, Wilson saw keys hanging on a set of hooks. He then walked towards the rear of the building, ending up in a small kitchen. Through the window of a back door, he saw a pickup truck parked in the back.

Wilson decided he would wait here about two hours and then leave. Once in Mandeville, he could find somewhere to hole up and kill some time. He would park the truck in some parking lot and walk to his next stop. Before he left Yokem's, he would wash up, get presentable, and be out of here before anyone questioned why the place was closed.

The plan was coming together. Wilson closed his eyes and leaned back, a grin of satisfaction spread across his face.

CHAPTER THIRTY-EIGHT
Analysis

Wong and Dozier were engrossed as they each scanned various pieces of information relating to the public search for Andre Waters and Doris Plaisance, and the private search for David Wilson. The contents contained the sighting of the woman and the boy in Memphis hours earlier, along with the recovery of the helicopter and a tranquilized Frank Johnson. The reports concluded with a documented observation of a Coast Guard vessel seeing a small jet, flying erratically at low altitude, heading out to sea over the Gulf of Mexico.

The interrogation of Screw Johnson revealed that a gun had allegedly been placed on him and that he was unaware that it was not a lethal weapon. Johnson had maintained that no discussion had ensued but that he thought he heard the woman muttering something about going to Texas, and then Mexico, as everyone would be looking for them to go to Louisiana.

Dozier began to squint. "What do you think, Charles? If they are heading to Texas, that could really mess up our plans."

Wong shook his head. "That man has had a bout of conscience. His file says that he supervised most of the boy's training. My guess is that he decided to help the boy and the woman and this is his way of trying to assist further. My feeling is that they are heading to Louisiana and are probably getting closer to achieving that goal by the minute. No, our plans stay the same. We focus our resources on the Waters' house."

Dozier rose from his chair and began to pace. "Do we set up road blocks at all?"

Wong swiveled in his chair. "I would just keep all local law enforcement on alert. We would need a confirmed sighting before that kind of strategy would be effective. Do we have phone taps on the Waters home in place?"

Dozier nodded affirmatively. "We do, but they have stopped using any kind of phone or e-mail. It's like they have gone into seclusion."

Wong answered quickly. "No doubt they have been bombarded by the media. I imagine I would do the same thing if I were in their situation. Let's shift our focus to David Wilson for a moment. "At this time we know we have no signal that we can track from Wilson's cell phone and that an aircraft fitting the description of our missing jet was seen over the Gulf of Mexico, correct?"

"Correct. There has been no confirmation of the plane going down. It could crash, or have crashed, anywhere in the Gulf by now." Dozier relayed the response in a monotone voice.

Wong pulled a manila folder out of his brief case. "I have the dossier on David Wilson. He has no college degree, yet served in Naval intelligence and has worked at various intervals for both the FBI and CIA. This information is more descriptive of a computer nerd than an assassin. Is there anything else I should know about him?"

Dozier sat back down. "I never worked directly with him, but the word on him was that his IQ was off the charts. He stands about six foot five, and if he caught people by surprise, it wouldn't be hard for him to pull this off. If we are to assume he took control of the aircraft he would have had to smuggle a weapon aboard the jet, kill the escorting agents along with his own man, and then force the pilot to change course."

Wong's eyes widened. He began to stroke his chin with his thumb and index finger. "We know that the Waters boy and he are related and that he conceived of the notion of exploiting the child's abilities after seeing him at a family function. We also know that when the boy bolted, all of his efforts to reacquire him failed. I also find a similarity in that the boy and the teacher captured a helicopter and Wilson in turn may have commandeered a jet. I think this has turned into some kind of warped competition. Wilson doesn't care about his career anymore or his country. He cares about his own intellectual superiority. I think he has become psychotic because he feels enraged at the thought that a boy only ten years of age with a mental disability could have outwitted him."

Dozier stared at Wong. "My God, that is quite an analysis."

Wong then got up. "I want you to pull all of your men away from the Waters home."

Dozier looked dumbfounded. "Do what?"

Wong moved around his desk and looked directly at Dozier. "Mr. Wilson is going to solve our problem. He is going to intercept the boy, kill him, and then we will apprehend our former colleague and close this case."

"Jesus, that is far-fetched. He may still be on the jet," Dozier replied, stunned.

"Is it? Is it any more far-fetched than what we have seen over the past twenty-four hours? David Wilson is not going to be caught off guard or become soft-hearted. He will shoot that boy on sight and probably everyone else. He will then flee the scene. Once we have confirmation that he has succeeded, we can covertly go about the business of apprehending him. There will be no media attention or cover up because no one knows of David Wilson's existence except those with the highest level of security clearance. Tell me, Al, do those jets come equipped with parachutes?"

"Yes, they do."

"I'm more than confident David Wilson is in Louisiana heading for the Waters house as we speak."

Dozier sat back and rubbed both hands through his hair. "You really think this can work?"

Wong was stone-faced. "It has to. All other means would lead to some kind of leak to the media with relentless investigations that would follow. If Wilson does kill the boy, we have the means to secure the required silence by those in the inner circle who would know what happened."

Dozier began to noticeably sag in his chair. He felt like a criminal. He had a grandchild not much younger than Andre. "How do we track down

Wilson? He's not going to hang around waiting for us."

Wong paced the room. "I think you are mistaken. I think he will come back to Washington believing he will be greeted as some conquering hero. If he does flee, the FBI or the CIA will find him."

CHAPTER THIRTY-NINE
A New Journey Begins

Jerome, Doris, and Tyrone all sat on the couch staring at the television. Andre was sitting on the floor lining up shot glasses he had found on a counter in Jerome's kitchen. The glasses were equally spaced and were aligned in a serpentine manner as they stretched across the living room floor. On the screen was the image of the convenience store clerk, describing his encounter with Doris and Andre.

"Whooo-weee, they is gonna be hot on the scent fo' shore," Tyrone bellowed. "We has to get moving now."

They all rose and moved outside to the van. Doris covered Andre with a blanket in the event a nosy neighbor, even at five-thirty in the morning, might find it odd that three African Americans might be traveling with a Caucasian child. They piled into the van. Tyrone started the engine and pulled off with Jerome right behind them.

Tyrone yelled in the back. "You know who this boy is now and where he lives. Why don't we just call his parents and just hand him over?"

"I thought of that, but I'm certain their phones are probably tapped. The authorities could get to us before the parents could," Doris replied.

Tyrone nodded. "You probably right. Okay, we gonna to do it the hard way."

The van moved out of the neighborhood. The morning sun was slowly rising. The hard scrabble neighborhood gave way to a street that was dotted with small retail shops. After a while, a large industrial park came into view. Tyrone negotiated the van into a fenced-in area with an expansive parking lot full of trailers and large trucks. He found a secluded spot shielded by a large container and came to a stop. Tyrone turned around. "I'm gonna load the rig first. When I come around, I'll stop. I want you and the boy to hustle into the rig. You got it?"

Doris nodded. Tyrone climbed out of the van. Doris pulled the curtain of the van's rear window back. In the distance, she could see Jerome parking.

Soon a large eighteen-wheeler appeared in view on the left of the storage container that hid his van. It braked and squealed to a halt, Tyrone making a summoning motion with his hand. Doris and Andre scurried from the van and headed towards the truck moving in unison at a fast trot. At the same time, Jerome was exiting his car. He moved around to the back of it and ripped the license plate off. He then ran towards the van. Doris and Andre covered the distance quickly and within moments, they were secure in the rear portion of Tyrone's cab. The large rig began to move and Jerome, now at the controls of Pugh's van, pulled into place behind it. Jerome had surveyed the area carefully and was satisfied that the pair had not been seen as they moved from the van to the truck. The two vehicles moved in tandem, eventually reaching I-55, and began heading south. If all went well, they would be approaching New Orleans by ten that morning.

CHAPTER FORTY
The Road to Confrontation

David Wilson listened carefully to the broadcast. He noted the time the clerk at the convenience store gave when he had seen Doris and Andre. Wilson then made notes on how long it would take Andre to reach Mandeville if he was not impeded.

By his calculations, the Rat could arrive at his familial home by early afternoon. He based his assumptions on his belief that the pair was still traveling by bus or car. He realized that with the media on alert, it would be more difficult for them to remain inconspicuous, but he could not delay any longer. He would have to make a move soon, as he wanted to be at the house well ahead of Andre's arrival. Before leaving, he again sifted through the desk in the office area and found some money in a small box in the drawer. He counted out four-hundred twenty-six dollars. He had a little over two-hundred on him, so he had enough cash to make ends meet for the immediate future. He had washed and ironed his shirt along with cleaning his under garments. He also had taken a shower. He had pressed his pants and wiped his shoes down. He was now presentable should he meet any people along the way.

He made note that no mention of the missing jet was made. Only government officials would be looking for him, which meant he had no worries as it pertained to local law enforcement. He needed the truck but would have to dispose of it quickly, as he was certain that the dead man on the floor a few feet away from him would be found within the next few hours. It was now eight-thirty. He wiped the room down thoroughly and grabbed the truck keys from the hook.

He exited the house and approached the parked truck. He settled in the driver's seat of the Chevy S-10, gripping the steering wheel with paper towels. He pulled out of the driveway and turned right.

His computer map mimicked the old man's instructions. He made a left turn on Hoffman Road. The winding road was scenic, with large trees blanketing it on either side. Soon the service road came into view. He turned right. Within minutes he was at its end, the interstate visible on his left.

As he reached the service road's end, Wilson saw the combination gas station and convenience store the old man had referred to. He turned left onto Highway 22 and then took the I-55 exit to Hammond. His map indicated that within a couple of miles he would intersect with Interstate 12, at which time he would follow it east until he came to the Mandeville-Covington exit, approximately twenty-two miles away.

All was going according to plan. After about fifteen minutes he crossed into St. Tammany Parish, then later over the Tchefuncte River. By the time his exit came into view, he had been driving a little over thirty minutes. He turned right, veering towards Mandeville. Almost immediately the Fairway Drive exit appeared. He angled the truck onto it and then turned left, back under the overpass that was US 190. As he reached the end of Fairway Drive, a large hospital came into view. He now had a place to dispose of the truck and he would be close enough to walk to the Waters' house.

Wilson parked the truck deep behind the hospital. He lowered the tailgate to obscure the license plate, hoping to delay any connection between it and the murdered man back in Ponchatoula, should his remains be discovered. He then walked around to the front of the hospital and entered through the main door. What better place to wait and watch the news. He was just another visitor and there was certain to be a cafeteria with a television. He could get something to eat and bide his time until he felt certain Andre was in reach.

Wilson stopped at the information desk and was directed down the hall to the cafeteria. He passed through the line, getting some breakfast. He then found a small table and watched as the Fox News Channel updated a breathless nation on the manhunt for the kidnapper and her helpless autistic victim.

Wilson ate slowly. He would show up at his cousin's house to comfort her as he had been in New Orleans on business. He tried to call, he would say, but could not get through. Oh, it would be so simple. Then once the deed was done he would take the Waters' car, head down to Houma, and persuade his mother to give him money so he could get a boat and get out of the country.

Wilson felt a tingle of excitement. Soon, very soon, he would be face to face with his nemesis.

CHAPTER FORTY-ONE
Louisiana

The large rig moved swiftly down I-55. Tyrone had brought a bag of fruit on board plus a small cooler of soft drinks. Andre dined on apples and bananas while drinking Pepsi.

Doris declined food but did sip on a Pepsi. She was all too familiar with this area. She had always planned to visit her old home state, but not like this.

They crossed the state line and were now in Louisiana. Signs indicated that they were passing near Kentwood. Tyrone began to cackle. "Hey boy, keep your eyes open. You might see Britney Spears." Tyrone was laughing harder referencing the pop star to her place of birth. "That Britney can shake it but I don't think she sings all that good. Now Beyoncé, that's a whole 'nother thing there."

Doris began to smile, affected by Tyrone's good humor. She then glanced at Tyrone's side view mirror. Tucked close by was Jerome in the van.

Miles passed quickly. Soon they saw signs for Hammond. The I-12 intersection would soon come into view. Doris didn't want Andre to see the interstate, for fear of another tantrum if he recognized it as the way to his house. Doris wasn't sure how to distract Andre. She decided to use a finger play.

"The wheels on the bus go round and round," Doris sang the words while rolling her wrists in front of her.

Andre beamed a broad smile. He watched her every move.

"The babies on the bus go wah wah wah," as Doris began rubbing her eyes like she was crying. Andre continued to smile and watch her.

Soon the truck was past the intersection and was now heading south on I-55. It approached an elevated section of the interstate. They would be passing over water, through Manchac, where Lake Pontchartrain and Lake Maurepas met. Finally, they would intersect with I-10 and from there to the Causeway.

Tyrone leaned his head back. "Doris, I'm going to take the LaPlace exit. There is a truck stop there. From there, you and the boy can get in the van with Jerome and head on your way."

Doris reached over and grasped Tyrone's shoulder. "I don't know how we can ever thank you."

Tyrone beamed a smile back at her. "Your husband is a good man. But I know he must be wanting a drink real bad by now. You be strong for him. I sure hope you all get that boy home."

Jerome was following close behind, his body quivering, with beads of sweat pouring down his face. He was dead tired, craving alcohol, and he was in physical pain. He watched as Tyrone put on his blinker and headed off the interstate. The truck stop was now in plain view. Tyrone eased the rig onto road and put his blinker on signifying a left turn.

As Tyrone entered the truck stop, he directed the rig to the far side of the convenience store located on the grounds. He noticed a St. John the Baptist Parish Sheriff's patrol car parked in front. Tyrone frowned. "Let's hope that deputy is still drinking his coffee."

Jerome pulled alongside. Doris wrapped Andre in a blanket and they got out of the truck. Doris waved silently at Tyrone before she and Andre got in the van with Jerome. Tyrone then pulled away, heading back towards the interstate.

Jerome looked blankly at Doris. "Baby, we need gas. Do you have some money?"

Doris looked shocked. She saw that Jerome was going through withdrawal. To make matters worse, she was now near her hometown. It was possible she or Jerome could be recognized. "Oh Jerome, yes I have money, but are you going to be okay? You look terrible." Doris' voice was filled with concern.

Jerome grasped her hand. "I'll be fine. Give me cash and I'll go pay inside. I don't think we should use a credit card. Keep the boy down."

Doris handed Jerome fifty dollars. He drove the van to a pump nearest the highway, got out and began filling the vehicle with gas. The pump clicked off. Jerome replaced the handle, then walked inside the station to pay. As he approached the register, a deputy passed by him. Noticing Jerome shaking slightly, he stopped. "Say man, are you all right?"

Jerome turned and faced the deputy, his face sweaty and his eyes blood shot. "Yes sir, I'm fine."

The deputy persisted. "You don't look so fine. You ain't on anything, are you?" The deputy was something of a stereotype. Large and big boned with a military haircut and what appeared to be a perpetually red face and neck.

Jerome managed a weak smile. "No sir, I have been up all night. You can see I don't smell of liquor. I just need some sleep. I'm on my way home now."

The deputy glared at Jerome and then turned and walked away.

Doris looked down, using peripheral vision to watch the deputy, first as he spoke with Jerome and then as he left the store. She had Andre seated in the van's rear, the blanket covering him.

The deputy got in his car and drove off, heading away from the interstate towards LaPlace. Jerome then came out and got back in the van. He let his head slowly drop onto the steering well. "Lord, that was close."

Doris rubbed his back with her hand, a tear strolling down her face. "Oh Jerome, you are so brave."

Jerome straightened up, as if Doris' words and touch were adrenaline. "Baby, it's time to get this lil' man back to his folks."

CHAPTER FORTY-TWO
A Trap is Set

David Wilson watched the news and was surprised that no new information was forthcoming on the manhunt for Doris Plaisance and Andre Waters. He was on his third cup of coffee and had peed once already. His watch said ten-thirty. He was now growing anxious. He had no way of knowing what progress Andre and Doris had made so far in their effort to get the boy to his home. He felt they should be getting closer by now. As such, he was grappling with what to do. Should he leave now? If he got to the Waters' house too early, he would eventually have to make a decision about what to do with Jenny and Mike. He also began to think about surveillance. Surely, the Waters' house is being watched. How would he manage an encounter with law enforcement?

Wilson couldn't sit in the hospital much longer. He had to do something. Andre was heading this way and if he had been caught, it would have made the news. He looked down at the table. This was the time to leave. He rose from the table and stepped away, carefully pushing the chair back in place. He then turned about and walked out of the cafeteria, heading towards the exit.

Wilson emerged through the door and found himself standing in front of the hospital entrance. He pulled from his pocket the map he made from the computer at the reptile farm. He saw that he had to walk down Fairway Drive until it ended at Westwood Drive. At Westwood, he would turn left and walk until he hit Dove Park Road. He would turn left on Dove Park and follow it to Orleans Avenue. The Waters house would then be on the left.

From his calculations, he was less than two miles away. He began to walk down the side of the road. It was warmer in Louisiana than in Illinois or Washington, and he soon began to perspire. He noticed quickly that there were no sidewalks and that he could appear conspicuous walking down the street in a suit.

He decided to be cheery and wave or smile at passing cars. He wasn't worried about being identified or appearing suspicious. No one knew who he was anyway. Besides, by this evening he would be on his way to Houma, and by tomorrow he would be heading for some Caribbean isle. He had money in the Grand Caymans in a numbered account. He would beat them all and laugh about it on some sunny beach.

Wilson reached Westwood Drive and found himself in the middle of a subdivision. The street was empty, the heat probably keeping people inside. As before, there were no sidewalks. Wilson wanted to avoid any contact with the local populace so he picked up his pace. Eventually he came to Dove Park Road. He turned left and was almost immediately turning onto Orleans Avenue. In the distance he saw a row of houses. At the end was a two story green Acadian-style house with a metal roof.

He reached the house. He saw a Jeep Cherokee parked in the driveway next to the house, and in the front of the house on a circular drive covered in aggregate was a Toyota Camry. Both Jenny and Mike must be home, he thought.

He scanned the long street. It was devoid of cars. He looked down all the driveways of the various houses. Cars were parked, but unoccupied. Could it be that his peers were so confident that they could intercept Andre that they did not bother to stake out his parent's home?

It was now or never. If there was someone out there, the only way he would discover that would be to approach the house and force their hand. Wilson walked past the Camry and mounted the steps onto the covered porch. He rang the doorbell.

A deep voice barked from inside. "Who is it?"

Wilson gathered himself. "Mike, it's me, David Wilson. I'm Jenny's cousin. I met you at my sister's wedding a few years back." Suddenly, a face appeared around the curtain shrouding the door's inlaid glass. It was Jenny. She unlocked the door and opened it.

"David, what are you doing here?" Jenny's face had a shocked look on it.

"I was in New Orleans on business. I have been following the story in the news so I thought I would just stop in and see how you were doing. May I come in?"

Jenny opened the door wider. "Of course. I'm sorry. This has just been a hard day." Jenny composed herself. "David, this is quite a surprise. You are the last person I would have expected to see. Please sit down. How is Aunt Maureen?"

Wilson sat on the couch with Jenny beside him. Mike was now back in his easy chair. He looked at Wilson, seemingly perplexed by his arrival. He nodded slightly and then turned his attention back to the television, which had the news on.

"Mother is fine, I think. I have been so busy I haven't called home in some time." Wilson realized that he hadn't fully prepared himself for a barrage of questions so he decided to try to direct the focus of attention away from himself. "So, any word other than what is on TV?"

Mike shrugged. "Not really. The media has finally begun leaving us alone and we haven't heard from any law enforcement as far as updates."

Jenny then chimed in. "We were told that the FBI was involved and that they wanted to see our son before we could."

Wilson sank back in the couch. "The FBI wants to see Andre? Are there any agents nearby?"

Mike looked off in the distance. "Perhaps. If they are, they must be in the trees or under rocks."

Wilson sat up. "How do you know the FBI wants to see him? Have you spoken with anybody from the Bureau?" His voice was heightened with excitement.

Mike began to ponder Wilson's interest in the FBI and his son's predicament. This was not the kind of conversation someone makes when consoling people. "No, David. We have not talked with anybody from the FBI."

Wilson now appeared almost agitated. "Then how do you know the FBI wants to see Andre?"

Mike listened to David's words. He noticed that his shirt was drenched with sweat and that his hair, while combed, had a greasy look to it. Mike found it odd that a relative that Jenny barely knew would suddenly just pop in on them and start asking all of these questions about the FBI. Something was peculiar about this visit and David's behavior. Mike decided to start asking some questions of his own.

"David, why are you curious about whether we know that the FBI wants to see Andre? Is there some point to all of this?"

Wilson looked away. "I was just trying to help, I guess. I'm concerned for you and Jenny."

Mike sensed Wilson was lying. Perhaps it came from his years in banking where you had to assess the risk in lending money to strangers. That instinct was working now and Mike began to feel angered by this intrusion on himself and his wife. Mike's tone was not hostile, but it was direct. "David, not to change the subject, but exactly what type of business brought you to New Orleans?"

Wilson was taken aback. "Uh, Mike, well, I thought you knew I was a consultant."

Mike kept probing. "I have met many consultants over the years. Their work fascinates me. What kind of consulting do you do?" The tone of Mike's voice was now bordering sarcastic.

Jenny became flustered with the tenor of the conversation between her husband and her cousin. "Mike, that's enough. David didn't come here to answer questions. He came to see us and see how we were holding up. I'm sorry, David."

Wilson managed a weak smile. "That's okay, Jenny. I know you both are on edge."

Jenny looked away. "David, I think Andre is trying to come home. I don't believe that teacher kidnapped Andre. I think she is trying to help him. The authorities are all wrong on this."

Wilson was amazed. How intuitive his cousin was. "Jenny, I'm sure there is more to this than meets the eye. There always is."

Mike then rose from his chair. "That's interesting that you would say that. What is your theory on all of this?"

Wilson became unnerved. "Mike, I don't have a theory. It was just a figure of speech."

Jenny chimed in as well, "Mike, stop that. What has gotten into you?"

Mike dismissed them both with a wave of his hand. He then moved slowly to his left and pulled back the sheet covering the inlaid window in the front door. "David, how did you get here? I don't see a car in the driveway."

Wilson could feel the color draining from his face. "I had a friend drop me off."

Mike sensed the uneasiness in Wilson's voice. "Really, you had a friend from New Orleans drive you across the Causeway, and just drop you off? If you are in New Orleans on business, why would you be free during the day? Shouldn't you be meeting with your client or something?"

Wilson became livid, his composure vanishing. "I have had enough of your stupid questions!"

Mike stared at David, looking him up and down. "You don't look to me like a guy who took an air conditioned car ride. You look like a guy who took a long walk in the sun wearing a hot suit. Just why in the hell are you here?"

Wilson began to rise from the couch but Mike continued on. "Jenny, why would a cousin you barely know show up out of the blue to console us when he didn't even attend his own father's funeral?"

Wilson pulled his gun out. "You just shut the fuck up and sit down." He moved closer to Mike, the gun pointing at his face.

Jenny was struck dumb, her mouth open, frozen with shock and fear.

Wilson's eyes were wide and bulging. Mike Waters had screwed up his plans with his questions and had forced him to play his hand earlier than intended.

Mike remained still, but was not done. "Jenny you were right, Andre is trying to come home. This animal took him. You always said your family thought he was some kind of government spy. He saw Andre at the wedding, and then a few weeks later Andre was gone. He's in our home because he knows Andre will be coming here too. He's asking questions about the FBI because they are probably looking for him as well."

Wilson swung his gun hand, stricking Mike hard in the face. Mike buckled but didn't fall. Wilson glared at Mike, snarling, "I'm going to shut you up permanently."

Mike placed his hand to his face, trying to stem the flow of blood from his brow, but his teeth were clenched and his eyes were shooting daggers at Wilson. Wilson began to think. He had to wait until Andre arrived and they were all together. If he shot them both now, it might alert the neighbors and the police could be called. Wilson wheeled and pointed the gun at Jenny, stepping back from Mike at the same time. "If you aren't afraid to die, perhaps you will have more concern for your wife."

Mike straightened up. His anger was overwhelming but he knew by the time he lunged for the gun Wilson could fire it and probably kill Jenny. He glared at Wilson. "Where do you want me?"

Wilson regained his composure. "Move to that wall and sit on the floor." The Waters' dining room flowed into the kitchen. A short wall divided the room. Mike moved over to the wall and slid his back down it until was seated on the floor.

Jenny spoke, her voice trembling. "Why did you do it, David? Why did you take my son away from me?"

Wilson glared at Jenny. "Why? Because he was perfect! The perfect thief! The perfect spy! This country is under siege by terrorists, gangsters, and deviants. We were losing. Losing! That boy, under my leadership, was helping us turn the tide. We made arrests, stopped bombings, saved lives, all because of his ability to steal information from under the very noses of the enemy. Then he finds a damn map and decides to go home. He betrayed his country. He betrayed me!" Wilson's voice was now at a fever pitch.

Jenny began to cry. "Betrayed his country? David, he's ten years old. My God, you are insane!"

"Shut up! Shut up! I'm not insane! I'm a visionary! That boy was a stroke of genius! My genius! He is going to pay for what he has done!"

As if some emotional bond connected them, Andre Waters' parents did not respond to the final outburst. Instinctively, they both realized that to further antagonize Wilson might result in dire consequences for one or both of them. And they had to stay alive until Andre got home.

Wilson moved carefully over to the kitchen table. He pulled a chair over and placed it by the front door so he could survey the front of the house. He then focused his eyes on Mike and Jenny, an eerie calm falling over him. "Don't worry. He won't suffer. It will be better this way. I, at least, offered him a life of service to his country. What use was he otherwise?'

Jenny lowered her head. What use was he? He was a human being, and deserved to live as much as anyone else. Mike sat still, but his rage had not subsided. Who was this bastard to judge his boy? Mike made up his mind that he was going to die before he allowed this maniac to kill his son.

Wilson checked his watch. It was close to noon. It shouldn't be much longer now.

CHAPTER FORTY-THREE
The Causeway

Jerome, Doris, and Andre were churning down I-10 heading towards New Orleans. They were on an elevated bridge called the Bonnet Carré Spillway, with water and marshland on either side of them. The Louis Armstrong International Airport was nearby, where many of the commercial airlines making their approaches seemed like they would land right on top of the cars beneath them.

Jerome was careful not to exceed the speed limit. He didn't want to draw attention to himself in any way. Doris tried to keep Andre close to her. They were both lying down in the back, out of sight, to minimize the possibility of either of them being identified by another motorist who might happen to glance their way.

"We probably should have laid low until dark. I feel like this is not a good idea traveling in the open like this." Jerome was fatigued, his voice weak.

Doris remained upbeat. "Traveling by day might be the last thing they would expect us to do."

"Doris, if we do make it across the Causeway, how will we find the kid's house?"

Doris was not sure how to answer that question. "Andre may very well show us. If not, we can stop at another gas station and I will call his parents from there. We would be close enough that they could probably get to us before the police could. I just hope they are listed in the phonebook and don't have their phone off the hook."

By now, the car had entered into the outskirts of New Orleans. They had just passed the Loyola exit, which meant they were now in the city limits of Kenner. Soon they would be in Metairie, a suburb of New Orleans, and the exit to the Lake Pontchartrain Causeway would be just a short distance away.

The interstate was full of cars, though traffic was moving briskly. Jerome had worried earlier about a wreck or construction delays but nothing like that was visible. They had passed the Veterans and Clearview exits. He carefully moved the van to the right lane and saw the first sign indicating the Causeway exit was next.

Jerome put his blinker on and got off the interstate. He stayed straight and then slowly shifted over another lane so he could head north. As the van moved in a tight bank, they headed up to the top of an overpass. The interstate was now beneath them. They merged again, passing over Veterans Highway. Lakeside Mall was on their left. Jerome remembered going there with Doris at Christmas the first year their son was born. Their Andre had his first picture with Santa Claus taken there. He remembered the little train the mall had set up and how their son had giggled as he rode in it.

The deep blue tint of the lake could be seen in the distance. Jerome steered the van to the far right lane and headed for the bridge.

Traffic heading to the Northshore was brisk but light. Jerome knew that most of the traffic at this hour was going north to south as commuters headed into the city to go to work.

They soon came up to the beginning of the bridge. As Jerome had stated hours earlier, tolls were now collected only on the northern side of the bridge to ease traffic flow.

Jerome slowed to the recommended speed of twenty miles an hour and passed through. The speed limit on the Causeway was sixty-five miles an hour and Jerome maintained it, staying in the right lane. The lake was like a blue piece of glass. For those who didn't cross the bridge regularly the ride could seem like an eternity. The Causeway was dotted with crossovers.

The bridge was patrolled by its own police force. Every mile was marked, which rather than making a person feel as if they were closer to the end, often had the effect of making one feel further away.

Doris had repositioned herself in the back of the van and had persuaded Andre to lie down on her lap. The ride had a familiar feel to the boy and he dozed off. Soon it was as if they were in the middle of an ocean. Neither the north nor south shores were visible, just a vast amount of water in every direction. They had been riding about fifteen minutes and were now just past the twelve-mile marker. Jerome began thinking they were halfway there. He looked in his rear view mirror and saw that Doris was asleep as well.

Jerome was exhausted. He had not slept at all at Tyrone's house and he had been driving nonstop since yesterday evening. All of that, combined with his withdrawal from alcohol and the nervousness of their situation, was beginning to be overwhelming. He nodded slightly then jerked awake with that sudden blast of fear that comes with almost falling asleep at the wheel.

More miles passed. The van moved over the drawbridge section, the northern shore of the lake now coming into focus. Jerome was fighting fatigue with all his might. He began to bite down on his bottom lip.

The van shook violently as it collided with the outside rail of the bridge. All the passengers awoke, including the driver.

"Jerome, what happened?" Doris' eyes were wide with fear.

"I'm sorry Baby, I fell asleep. I have been try…" Jerome's voice cut short as he saw the flashing lights in his rear view window. "Oh Christ, Doris, it's a cop! What should I do?"

Doris felt as if all her muscles in her body had gone soft. "Jerome, we can't outrun him. Just pull over and we'll deal with it together."

"I'll have to wait until the next crossover. Damn, we were almost at the end."

The two vehicles moved in single file. The next crossover was just ahead. They were only three miles from the end of the bridge. They switched lanes and slowed, both vehicles turning into the crossover.

Jerome pulled to a stop and cut the engine off. A radio from the patrol car sent out a stern message, "Please step out of the vehicle."

Jerome was seated with both hands on the steering wheel. This was a practice he had learned to appease law enforcement officials, as he knew they would be able to see his hands and not feel threatened.

Officer Bernie Karl stepped out of his patrol car. He slowly approached Jerome, who had exited from the driver's seat slowly and was now standing next to the van.

"License please." Jerome dug out his wallet, found his license and handed it to Karl. "You veered into the railing hard. Have you been drinking?"

"No sir. I'm just real tired. I have been up all night."

Officer Karl was looking at the license and then the car. "Your license is for Louisiana but the van has Mississippi plates.

Karl stared back at the license. He turned back and faced Jerome. "What's in the back?"

Jerome tried to remain calm. "Nothing sir."

"Mind if I take a look?" Without waiting for a response he grabbed the handle of the sliding side door. With a jerk he opened it wide.

Suddenly Karl recoiled in pain. Andre had moved to the door and the instant it opened he had jabbed his index and middle fingers into the deputy's eyes.

As the officer stumbled backwards, Andre jumped in the air and drove his right foot into the solar plexus of the stricken deputy. Karl let out a hard exhale and crumpled to his knees, his head bowed.

Andre raced around the front of the van, glancing backwards at Jerome. Doris rushed out of the side door and affixed her eyes on Andre. Andre then gazed at her, as if for the final time. He grabbed the rail of the cross over and leapt over the side, dropping down feet first towards the lake below.

"Andre!" Doris screamed. She bolted to the railing and looked over. She saw nothing. It was as if the boy had disappeared into thin air. Doris then moved to the other side of the van. She saw the stricken police officer struggling to get up. He was having trouble catching his breath and he had one hand over his eyes, his face still contorted in pain.

Doris moved towards him and both she and Jerome helped him to his feet. “Officer, we aren’t going to give you any trouble. Please just take us to the nearest police station and we will tell you everything we know.”

Karl began to peer about. His voice was almost inaudible as he uttered his question. “Where is the boy?”

Doris remained calm. “I saw him run down the bridge heading south. You probably need to put out an alert. He is autistic and could get himself or someone else hurt.”

Karl quickly handcuffed Doris and Jerome and then led both of them to his car, placing them securely in the back seat. He then began using his radio, relaying the false information Doris had given him, never bothering to move to the southern span of the bridge and see if Andre was heading in that direction.

Doris was in crisis mode. Andre had to swim a distance of over three miles and she had to buy him time to make it across.

The temperature of the water was cold compared to the air outside. Upon entering the water, Andre remained submerged and quickly took his shoes off. He then began to move towards a concrete pillar, one of many that supported the massive Causeway.

Andre reached the pillar, emerged for a second, gulped air, and then used his feet to push off towards the next pillar. He glided under the water kicking his feet and using his arms in a sweeping motion that was similar to passing through a thick brush in the woods. He continued this process, moving from pillar to pillar, focused only on getting to the shore. Andre had spent hours in pools and routinely had swam great distances as part of his training.

Officer Karl was behind the wheel of his car, siren blaring and lights flashing. The Causeway Police sub-station was located next to the Northshore tollbooths. On the other span, police cars could be seen heading south.

The patrol car reached the edge of the bridge and made a sharp left, cutting across to the other side and into the parking lot of the Causeway Police substation. Two more officers met the car to lead Doris and Jerome inside. They passed a reception desk and were led to a back room and sat at a table. A middle-aged plump man with gray hair and glasses approached and sat down before them.

"My name is Sergeant Buchanan Prechter." His voice was calm and not threatening. In his hand was an all-points bulletin with two photographs. One was a black woman. The other was of a white boy. "Are you Doris Plaisance?"

Doris looked up, her face almost serene. "I think you know that already."

Prechter glanced back at his paperwork then raised his eyes, locking them on Doris. "You and your companion here were heading towards that boy's home, weren't you? Is there something you'd like to tell me?"

Doris stared back. "I will tell you everything but first I need to know, have you called the FBI?"

Prechter grinned. "Not yet, but it is on my list of things to do."

Doris was unmoved by the sarcasm. "I will tell you everything if you wait until I am finished before you call the FBI."

Prechter frowned. "Madam, you are not in any position to cut deals. That kid has probably drowned by now or about to be picked up by one of my men. You could be facing a murder charge of some sort on top of kidnapping."

Doris smiled. "Sergeant, that boy is alive and you won't find him. Your officer that brought us in saw firsthand what he is capable of. I need your assurance not to call the FBI because I'm trying to save the child's life."

Prechter scratched his head. He had been in law enforcement all his life and could tell when someone was not telling the truth. This woman was telling the truth.

"Okay, you got it. I won't call anybody until after you have made your statement." Prechter summoned over a woman and whispered in her ear. Lacey Stuart left the room. In less than three minutes, she returned with a video camera.

Doris relayed the whole events of the past day and a half. The office slowly filled up with personnel from the Causeway Police, all mesmerized by what they were hearing. Prechter shuffled through various reports he had, matching the sequence of events to Doris' story. Doris finished and the room was silent. Another officer entered the room. He approached Prechter with two tennis shoes.

"Sarge, this is all we found. We are getting some boats out to begin dragging the lake but there is no sign of the kid."

Doris smiled. She glanced at her watch. It had been almost an hour since Andre had jumped over the side. "Sergeant, Andre is heading home. You have to get officers to his house to protect him and his family, and you can't call the FBI."

Prechter pushed back from the table. "Lacey, please get Fred Erwin on the phone. The rest of you are now officially under a gag order. The media will be snooping around soon enough. If this leaks I'll have someone's ass on a platter!"

Prechter turned his attention back to Doris and Jerome. "I'm going to lock you both up while we sort this out. I would normally give you a phone call, but I guess you would rather wait?"

"Yes, I would," Doris replied. "Just get to that child's house. His life depends on it."

CHAPTER FORTY-FOUR
The Race for Home

Andre emerged from the water to the far right of the bridge. He moved up a small sandy embankment and broke into a fast fluid gait.

Barefoot and dripping wet, he was moving with purpose. He had taken forty-five minutes to swim the three miles, but did not appear fatigued as he hit the shore. He knew exactly where he was and was now fueled on adrenaline.

He passed quickly down the street dissecting the Mariner's Cove office complex. Soon he came to the East Causeway approach. He crossed quickly, darting between the slow moving cars that were now commonplace in this community swollen by rapid population growth. He moved down the access road past a gas station and a retail shopping center. The main Causeway approach was to his left, but cars breezed by, not seeming to notice the young boy jogging down the access road.

He came to St. Ann Street and turned right. He passed more offices and a large apartment complex. The road curved left. He soon found himself at the intersection of St. Ann and US 190. He stepped off the road and began to catch his breath. This intersection was heavily trafficked and crossing it would be difficult on foot. A signal light was controlling the vehicle flow. St. Ann was on his left, with US 190 in front of him.

The light turned green. Seeing the cars stopping, Andre bolted. A large Lincoln Navigator was turning left from the other direction on St. Ann. Andre jumped and skidded over the hood, his rear end making a squeaking noise that was drowned out by the squeal of the Navigator's brakes. Andre landed in full gallop and sprinted across the other side. He was now on Asbury Drive, as the street name had changed, and he was moving over the gravel-encrusted shoulder of the road. He showed no pain as his bare feet pounded over the uneven surface. He passed a church and then came to another street.

He was now at Sharp Road. He turned right. His body was upright as he ran, his legs moving in short rapid movements as he propelled himself down the road. He passed some subdivisions but then the entrance to Westwood Estates came into view. He crossed to the other side of the street and entered the development.

At that moment, Prechter was talking with Fred Erwin. Erwin himself was going to accompany his deputies to the Waters' household.

Prechter exhaled. "Fred, what should I do about the teacher and her husband?"

Erwin responded. "Just hold them. Once I get to the boy's house and secure the situation, I'll get back to you."

Erwin's radio chirped. He clicked on it and listened patiently as the dispatcher spoke. "Sheriff, a kid matching the description of Andre Waters almost caused an accident on US 190 east near Asbury and St. Ann."

Erwin acknowledged the call and then spoke aloud. "That intersection is about a mile from his house. We have to move out."

CHAPTER FORTY-FIVE
End Game

Andre ran down Westwood Drive, veering right then left, as it straightened out. The street was practically deserted. The surroundings so familiar, as he and his family had used this street all the time. His muscles were tightening as they filled with lactic acid but he ignored the pain and his pace stayed constant. He eventually came to Dove Park Road and he stopped. He breathed in and out, rapidly at first, then more slowly. He walked deliberately onto Dove Park, turned left, and then began to jog lightly as the street veered right and became Orleans Avenue.

Andre moved down the left side of the road, his house now visible in the distance. He got within a block and then stopped. He cocked his head back and forth slowly, as if listening for a distant sound. He then ran to the rear of the neighbors' house and opened their back gate. He entered their back yard, and scaled the fence that divided his house from theirs. He dropped into his own yard and surveyed it. His swing set and gym were still there. Nothing was different. He then moved slowly towards the back deck that led to a set of steps that ended at the kitchen door. Andre peered through the window in the door. He saw David Wilson sitting on a dining room chair near the front door, a gun aimed at something he could not see.

Ducking below the window he slowly turned the back door knob. It was unlocked, but the door was always hard to open. He knew it would make a loud squeak if he tried to go in. Andre scrambled down the steps back into his yard. In previous assignments, Andre relied on his repetitive training, sorting through various scenarios, forming images in his mind. He became frustrated as he had nothing to reference as a means to enter the house undetected.

Andre scrambled back to the edge of the yard and squatted down against a tree. He began to rock back and forth flicking at his ears, his face contorted in anguish. He then began a process of recall. He began drawing down on his memories of past missions. He also began drawing on things that had happened to him at his house.

Loud noises bothered Andre. It was his weakness. Harsh or sudden sounds reverberated through him, causing him to grab his ears. The metal roof on his house was particularly noisy. A tree branch or pinecones that shook free during storms would often strike the roof with incredible force. Andre's room was upstairs and the noise would be particularly acute from up there.

He stopped rocking as his eyes fixated on dozens of pinecones scattered about the yard, residue of the many pine trees that were planted back there.

He rose up slowly and carefully selected several large pinecones that were hard and still bore a green tint. Those he could not hold he piled neatly at his feet. He gazed up at the metal roof. He reared back and began to send the pinecones one at a time upward towards the roof of the house. As they fell on the roof, a loud sound erupted. The sound repeated itself as Andre tossed increasingly more pinecones onto the roof. Each time a pinecone landed a loud noise erupted. From the perspective of Andre Waters, if the noise was painful for him it would be that way for David Wilson too.

Wilson, initially startled, rose to his feet. The noise appeared to be coming from the front of the house. He tried to look out the window while still maintaining his line of vision on Mike and Jenny. They both had now came to the same realization. Andre was outside. Mike realized it was now or never.

Mike rose to his feet. Wilson turned abruptly and faced him, raising his gun hand at the same time. Mike changed his expression as if something had caught his eye to the right of Wilson. Wilson took the bait, lurched his head to the side, and immediately pulled the sheet back on the inlaid window in the front door. Mike then lunged forward. Wilson turned back around just in time to see Mike crashing into him. Both men fell to the floor, Wilson's gun falling from his grasp.

Andre immediately came through the back door. He saw his father and Wilson struggling, with his mother screaming from the other side of the room. Suddenly, Wilson maneuvered himself on top of Mike. He grabbed the gun from the floor and viciously clubbed Andre's father in the head.

Before Wilson could move again, Andre had launched himself onto his back. Andre's pick was in his hand and with a single movement, he stabbed Wilson in his gun hand, causing the weapon to fall to the floor. Then he swiftly moved the pick upwards, partially inserting it into Wilson's ear.

"NO!" The sound roared from the small boy. "NO!" It was repeated just as firmly. If Wilson so much as moved a muscle, the pick could be shoved into his brain.

Wilson was stunned and angry. Andre could talk!

"Now Andre, you know I wouldn't hurt your Daddy." Suddenly, Wilson fired his right arm up. It drove Andre's arm and pick upward, but not before gashing the inside of Wilson's ear. Wilson then elbowed the small boy in his midsection causing him to fall back to the ground, doubled over on the floor.

Wilson stood up, blood flowing from his ear. "You little bastard. I'm going to kill you!" Andre, holding his midsection with one hand, began to crawl towards the dining area as Wilson stood over him, his face flushed with rage.

Suddenly another voice rang out. "You step away from my baby or I'll send you to Hell!" Jenny Waters, frozen in fear before, had her maternal instinct in full force as she watched her cousin strike her child. She had moved across the room and retrieved the gun, which she now had pointed directly at her son's attacker. Another sound was now present. Sirens were wailing and getting closer. "David, I mean it! Move away from my son!"

Wilson also heard the sirens. He turned slowly and faced Jenny. The right side of his face and neck was drenched in blood and his eyes were now thin slits. "You bitch! You don't have the nerve!"

He stepped towards Jenny and she fired. The bullet hit Wilson in the right shoulder and sent him falling backwards, crashing into the dining table. He gathered himself and began to move forward again, Jenny fired again, hitting Wilson in the throat.

St. Tammany Parish Sheriff's squad cars filed onto the Waters' property. Led by Fred Erwin, a gauntlet of law enforcement ascended the Waters' porch. Erwin banged on the door. "Mike, Jenny, its Fred, open up!"

A fatigued voice responded. "Hang on." The door slowly unlocked. Mike Waters, his face bloodied, moved to the side so Erwin and the other officers could file in. On the floor lay a motionless David Wilson in a pool of blood. Also on the floor, near where the dining room and kitchen converged, was Jenny, cradling her son in her arms.

CHAPTER FORTY-SIX
The Reckoning

White House Chief of Staff R.J. Naus entered the room. Already seated were Charles Wong, Al Dozier, and Coleman Tate. Naus looked frail and drawn. It was obvious that he had been in meetings all afternoon. He was still amazed that the National Security Advisor, Director of the FBI, and the head of Homeland Security were all involved in this national nightmare.

"I have called all three of you here today at the request of the President. This afternoon, David Wilson was taken into custody in Louisiana by the St. Tammany Parish Sheriff's Office, after attempting to kill Andre Waters and his family. This action occurred after Doris Plaisance, the woman traveling with the Waters boy, was apprehended on the Lake Pontchartrain Causeway linking New Orleans with St. Tammany Parish. Her statement of the day's events led the local authorities to the Waters household where Wilson was found with gunshot wounds in his shoulder and throat."

All three men became queasy and weak at the same time. Naus continued. "The President has been in discussions with the Louisiana Congressional Delegation, which had been called this morning after Ms. Plaisance had issued her statement to local law enforcement." Naus took off his glasses and wiped them. "As you can see, we have an extremely delicate situation here."

Wong spoke first. "What exactly is it that you require of us?"

Naus looked up, irritated. "Require of you? Why Charles, we require nothing from you. This audience is to apprise you of what steps are being taken to fix this awful mess that you three have allowed to take place."

Naus began to pace. "Mr. Wilson is going to be tried in a military court for the deaths of the three men on the plane he hijacked. The murder we think he committed in Ponchatoula, Louisiana, will remain unsolved."

Tate grew nervous. "Wilson might talk to the press."

Naus looked away. "Mr. Wilson was shot in the throat by the boy's mother. He will be in protective custody, but I doubt he will be making any statements anytime soon." Naus then glared at Coleman Tate. "I feel pity for Charles and Al as they were trying to get control of a bad situation, but for you, I feel nothing but disgust."

Naus was now on the other side of the room. He grabbed a pitcher and poured some water into a glass on the table. "We are going to relocate the boy and his family. There has been too much publicity and obviously the scandal that could be created by all of this is beyond description. The Waters family may also still be in danger, considering the type of work you had that child doing. As such, we are going to have to support and protect them the rest of their lives and the citizens of this country are going to have to foot the bill. We are also going to relocate Doris Plaisance and her husband in a similar fashion."

Naus began to pace again, taking sips of water. "Tate, I know you have been relieved of your duties. Wong, you and Dozier will remain in your current roles for now, but be warned that any inappropriate actions by either of you will result in dire consequences. Essentially, all of you have to develop acute amnesia regarding this incident."

Wong looked off in the distance. "What kind of consequences?"

Naus did not hesitate. "All of you would be arrested for attempted murder, accessories to murder, treason, and any other charges we can think of."

Dozier stood up. He gazed at the room's occupants. "You know what? I am fine with all of this. I'm happy as hell that kid made it. He deserved to go home and we are getting what we deserve. God bless him."

CHAPTER FORTY-SEVEN
A New Life

Jenny, Mike, and Andre exited the transport vehicle. All three were sporting different hair colors, part of the effort to hide them in plain sight. They were in front of a large office building located at the Belle Chasse Air Force Base. A smiling man with blond hair and a cherubic face approached them, his hand extended. "Welcome to Belle Chasse. I'm Jack Greenleaf, an envoy from Washington. We just have a bit of housekeeping before we get you three on your flight."

Greenleaf turned and began to walk the Waterses towards the entrance of a large hangar. He was making small talk but then his voice took a serious tone. "I know that nothing can replace the past five years and that your government is now asking you to make additional sacrifices. However, we have made numerous arrangements that we hope you will find to be acceptable."

He then showed Jenny a picture of a gated estate situated on what appeared to be a hill. A grove of orange trees could be seen in the distance. "Jenny, we found you a beautiful house with a swimming pool, horses, and other amenities. Your government stipend will take care of all your financial needs. You, Mike, and Andre can move about freely as long as you maintain your new identities and avoid Louisiana."

A broad grin crossed Jenny's face. "Is it near …"

Before she could finish, Greenleaf began to smile. "Yes, Jenny, you and your family will be less than thirty minutes from Disney World."

Disney World! Their favorite family vacation spot! Andre had already been there twice before the abduction. It was the only preference she offered when asked about where the family would be willing to relocate to. Greenleaf continued to talk. "We will need to know and approve many of your movements but your full time security will assist with that. Andre's life could still be in danger because of the work he did while he was with Homeland Security. You and Mike understand the precautions we are taking and why?"

Mike and Jenny nodded in agreement. They would be guests of the government in a gilded cage, but at least Andre would be safe. Greenleaf led them to a room in the hangar. He turned to Jenny and Mike. "There are two people I would like you to meet."

Seated at a table were Doris and Jerome. Andre spotted Doris and bolted towards her. She rose from the table and met him halfway, grabbing him in a bear hug. "Oh you sweet baby! You finally made it home."

Jenny walked towards them. Doris released her hold on Andre and looked at Jenny. "My name is Doris Plaisance."

Jenny looked at her with moist eyes. "I know exactly who you are." She then embraced Doris, crying softly on her shoulder.

Mike walked over and hugged Jerome. Andre stood up and looked at both couples, appearing confused. His head slowly cocked from one side to the other.

Greenleaf then spoke again. "Jenny, Mike, I would like you to meet the man who will coordinate your security." Entering from another room was Screw Johnson. Andre smiled broadly.

Greenleaf introduced Screw to the Waterses and was himself embraced by both parents, as they had later learned his role in Andre's journey. Screw then reached into his pocket and handed Andre a Twix, then turned to face Jenny and Mike. "I can live the rest of my life and never make up for the pain I caused you both. I want you to know that as long as I live, no harm will ever come to any of you, even if it means my own life. I swear this to both of you."

The Waterses nodded in silent agreement. In the background, a helicopter was in position, its rotors moving rapidly. Screw reached down and with one arm hoisted Andre in the air. Andre put his arms around his neck. He stared at Johnson and without warning, a monotone sound emerged. "Screw."

Johnson beamed a broad smile.

CHAPTER FORTY-EIGHT
Full Circle

The Federal Correctional Institute in Oakdale, Louisiana, is a seventeen-hundred bed facility classified as minimum security. Located between the cities of Alexandria and Lake Charles, Oakdale was a town in decline and the prison was one of its few economic drivers. The facility is managed by the Federal Bureau of Prisons and has some notoriety as the place of incarceration for both a former Louisiana Congressman and Governor.

Despite the prison's designation, one prisoner in particular was subject to intense scrutiny. He had killed four people at close range on a private jet. Two were FBI agents. The prisoner was David Wilson.

Wilson did not get a trial. He was all set to go to a SuperMax facility, have the key thrown in a hole, then the hole filled. That was until Wilson revealed that he had computers on timers set up in an array of locations. Computers that would flood the internet with all the mission details associated with Andre Waters if a kill code was not submitted prior to the timers expiring.

Wilson demanded a low security federal facility and that was what he got. He knew there were limits to which he could push the government. Even with his apparent leverage, incarceration was unavoidable. The caveat was that if anything did show up on the internet, his deal would be revoked. Was Wilson bluffing? No one in the FBI or the West Wing was willing to roll the dice on that possibility. The other condition was that Wilson would be jailed under a false name. As far as the world knew, he had been killed by Jenny Waters with a gunshot to the throat.

Wilson was kept away from the general population, which suited him. He was restricted from all electronic devices, including television, but was allowed books and newspapers. He ate and exercised alone. The irony was that he was back in Louisiana. Even more ironic was that Oakdale was the childhood home of Jenny Waters' mother. Even imprisoned, the specter of Andre Waters loomed over David Wilson. His voice had returned, but it was scratchy, and at times his words were indecipherable. His wounds, and the fact that he was now trapped in the very state he had sought to escape years ago, plagued him. It was the final insult as a result of his perceived treachery of the Rat.

Wilson was walking within the confines of the outdoor exercise area. He had the space to himself. His walk was more of an amble. This was when he spent his time planning. He had no parole, because technically he was never sentenced. He was off the grid. His only way out of Oakdale was escape. Even if he was able to get out, he would have to find Andre, and Andre was off the grid, too. They could not implant a chip in Andre because he would dig it out of his skin. That was part of the reason the Rat was initially able to get away from Brooks and Myers.

Wilson's face broke out in a wide grin. Andre did not have a chip, but all of Wilson's former agents did. Screw Johnson had a chip. During Wilson's transportation to Oakdale, he overheard the agents assigned to him discussing the security detail for Andre Waters. This breach of protocol was welcome news. Wilson now knew that Johnson was responsible for Andre's safety. Wilson also was banking on the fact that Johnson was operating under the assumption that he was dead. When he escaped—and he *would* escape—capturing someone who no longer existed would be a huge challenge. As far as David Wilson was concerned, it was not a matter of *if* he got to Andre, only a matter of *when.*

AFTERWORD

When I was eleven years old, my father passed away suddenly. I was too young to lose my most important male influence and it was a source of distress to me for many years. I sought out others to fill that void but unfortunately, while many did their best, it became apparent as I grew older that for me my father was irreplaceable.

I soon made a promise to myself that when I became a father I was going to recapture all those moments I missed with my own dad, especially if I had a son or sons. I also vowed not to be a pushy dad when it came to extracurricular interests. Just because I played sports, particularly basketball, was not going to mean that my children had to. I wanted to be supportive of the interests they had, as it was their life and happiness that was paramount.

What I wrote in the prologue was very similar to the experiences I had with two psychiatrists after my oldest son was missing milestones. When your child is diagnosed with a profound disability, it hits you on two fronts. It causes concern about their future and it destroys any plans you had for that same future. Whatever life you imagined was now irrevocably changed. To have two children afflicted is beyond description.

Like many parents with reasonable resources, we sought the best care possible for our boys. We did ABA, early intervention, diet changes, tried speculative treatments like secretin, which was a pig hormone that was allegedly a miracle cure. All had no effect on my sons. It was at that point that the hard truth sank in. My sons were profoundly autistic and intellectually disabled, and would be that way for life.

I found that special needs parents were often sorted into categories. There were those who committed their lives to caring for their child or children in their home. There were parents who felt they could find a cure and immersed themselves into that mission. For some, a group setting was important so they could discuss their challenges and concerns with other parents and caregivers. My goal from the day I learned of their diagnosis was to create or find an environment where they were healthy and happy and could reach their potential. I didn't want to dwell on what we didn't have or what could have been and I didn't want to rule out any care options that could best meet their needs. Whatever path was chosen, it had to be what their mother and I felt was best for them, not necessarily what was best for us.

Our home life was a disaster. One or more of the boys was always awake. One or more were always having behaviors, often self-injurious, and the school system we were in, as highly regarded as it was, could not provide the structure they needed to learn. They needed a twenty-four hour, seven days a week routine, and we could not provide that in a home setting.

I was very much against sending my boys to a care facility. For a guy like me, it was waving the white flag. The boys' mother won me over by saying we could give it a year and if we saw no progress bring them home. I then did some psychology on myself. I said this was no different than a wealthy family sending their child to an exclusive boarding school or even college.

The decision twenty-one years later has proven to be a good one. My boys are now young men and are happy, well adjusted, and cared for. We have taken numerous vacations with them over the years, and I even hit some milestones I thought I would never achieve, such as going to sporting events with them, the very same kind of events I went to with my own father before he passed away. More importantly, they have a home for life.

However, in the early years after we made the decision to enroll them, I was riddled with grief. Even though my life had gotten easier, and they were making progress, I missed them terribly. We were three hours away from them and brought them home every other weekend. Fridays and Sundays were six hour roundtrips. The boys always enjoyed car rides and for them it was only a three-hour journey one-way, but for their mother and me, it was exhausting and challenging.

About two years after they left home, I had to find a way to manage my grief. Somehow, I wanted to take this experience and turn it into something positive. I wanted to honor them and reflect the love I had for them. At first, I was going to write a story about my experiences as a special needs parent, both good and bad, but that in itself was painful. I didn't want to relive all of that again, so I took a different approach.

I decided to write a book with action, love, desperation, drama, resolve, and of course a happy ending. I know now, and knew it then, that I was no author. I had no delusions of grandeur. I just wanted to take an experience that had been draining and painful and turn it into something joyful and positive.

I tinkered with the book off and on for close to two decades. I had it edited a few times and critiqued by friends, family, and professionals. Finally, when I saw my sixtieth birthday rapidly approaching I decided it was time to do something. So I began to put chapters on my blog. To my surprise, those that read it seemed to enjoy it.

As chance would have it, a few months ago I toured the local facility for the Louisiana Association for the Blind. They had a printing division called L.A.B. Printing and Office Supplies. They also would do graphics and editing. Because of Libby Murphy, Brandy Garison, Alison Young, Jessica Mercer, and Marcus Mebes, my little book is now in print.

The characters in my book for the most part are based on real life people I have met. Andre Waters is the composite of both of my sons; although I will admit, my youngest one has the more dominant traits.

His nickname was in fact the Rat, because his mother did really find a stash of Fig Newtons in his room.

There are those who don't approve of artistic license with the autistic condition but if my book is read enough by that many people that it invites that kind of scrutiny then I will welcome it with open arms.

If by chance through the miracle of medical breakthroughs my boys ever do become self-aware they will have a little monument from their dad as a testament to how much I love them. With that said, they are my role models now regardless. No two young men operate on a day-to-day basis within the boundaries established by the Golden Rule better than them.

MCW